UNDERCOVER

A
NOVEL

BY

Sir Patrick Bijou

Copyright

Dedication

To all the individuals I have had the opportunity to lead, be led by, or watch their leadership from afar, I want to say thank you for being the inspiration and foundation of my life.

And so, I dedicate this book to a special lady and friend, Dame Kitty Suiyan Chen for her unfailing support and trust in me.

About the Author

Sir Patrick is a dynamic Investment banker, Fund Manager, and REDEMPTION JUDGE for the International Court of Justice and International Criminal Courts, he is also a published Author.

Sir Patrick's journey into content writing has allowed him to become an exceptionally motivated and enthusiastic author and professional communicator. Experienced in both proactive campaign-driven and responsive communications.

He lives and writes from the United Kingdom and is the author of several books in finance and fiction, UNDERCOVER is his third novel.

Many experiences have influenced his diverse writing prowess. In truth, he is a citizen of the world, and this dramatically affects his writing.

So, if you are already a fan of mine, I appreciate you. If you are not yet one, then what are you waiting for? Read a book and then read some more. I create characters that resonate with you and infuse life into all I write.

CHAPTER 1

Captain James Hendricks scowled at the Miami Police detectives, sitting across from him is Detective Levan Harris, the younger of the two, opened the file and flipped through photographs while his partner, Detective Carlos Zac, summarized the plan for the fourth time.

"I know it's risky," Espinoza said. "I know we've already lost one officer and two informants while trying to infiltrate the Las Casas organisation."

"Without a goddamned trace," Hendricks narled. "And without producing a scintilla of admissible evidence."

"This is our best chance to get close to the target,"

Zac countered "All she has to do is to plant the bug and get out."

"How reliable is this information?"

"I told you it's good, He has never lied to me or withheld anything useful not even once."

"What do you have on him?"

"Three parole violations. If we take him in, he's going away for life."

"Can you vouch for him, Harris?"

"I can't attest to his reliability, Captain, but I was the one who caught him moving product, so I am certain of his motivation." Harris pulled the informant's rap sheet from the file and handed it to Hendricks. "I don't know if he would lie, but he has tangible reason to cooperate."

"You two do realize; I hope that if anything goes wrong, then your careers are as good as over," Hendricks said "We have concurrent jurisdiction with the Feds in coastal waters, The Coast Guard, the FBI, the DE, and ICE will be all over our asses if you fuck this up. I won't be able to save you hell, I won't be able to save myself."

"Relax, Captain, relax," Zac responded "We've covered all the bases."

"I don't like it," Hendricks wipes his brow. "Does it have to be a fucking cadet?"

"No one else could pass," Harris answered. "Every woman who works at Renee's is under 25, has a rock hard body, and she is gorgeous. We don't have a detective young enough or pretty enough to get inside."

"How about a uniformed officer? We have over seventy female officers in this department at least one of them has to be hot enough, you can't tell me they all belong in the K-9 unit."

"Captain, we have a lot of attractive women working in the department as a organization, this size should be reasonable enough to have," Harris answered. "But there are none who are both young enough and sexy enough, not a single one. If we send somebody who doesn't meet the profile, she'll be made immediately, and probably our informant too, we can't take that chance."

"I don't like it."

"Just talk to her," Espinoza pleaded, "talk to her first, and then decide."

"I'll talk to her, but I can tell you right now I'm going to say no, the risk is too much." "I'll go get her, "Harris stood up and walked toward the door "one second."

Hendricks reached for the file and reviewed the notes. He looked at the informant's mug shots and rap sheet, and then pulled out the surveillance photographs, the most recent of which were two years old. He closed the file and stroked his goatee just as Harris returned with a young woman wearing a police cadet's uniform.

Despite tailoring designed to render the clothing as sexless and unappealing as possible, the shapely young woman looked stunning in the pressed blue uniform, her small breasts stood up firm and proud while a hint of nipple protruding through her shirt emphasised her femininity.

Her long legs were covered by creased blue pants that failed to hide the swell of her hips and the round curves of her ass. Her auburn hair was tied up and pinned tight against her head. She wore no jewellery or make-up on her golden skin, light smattering of freckles on her cheeks and nose made her appear even younger than her twenty-two years.

"Captain Hendricks," Harris said, "I present to you Cadet Dana Lvarado."

Hendricks stood up and extended his hand a low whistle escaped his lips as he eyed the woman up and down.

Harris turned to the young woman "Cadet Lvarado, Captain Hendricks."

Lvarado took the older man's hand and gave it a firm shake.

"Be seated," Hendricks said, "Let's get this over with soI can get on with my day." "Tell me about yourself, Lvarado."

"Well, Captain, where would you like me to start? How about, where were you born?"

"Here in Miami, Sir I'm a second generation Cuban-American. My father is from Havana, my mother is an American."

"Go on."

"Yes, Sir I graduated from Hialeah High. After that, I attended Florida International University where I majored in Criminal Justice, I entered the academy right out of school and I hope to be a detective, and I will eventually go to an law school so I can become a prosecutor."

"You must look damn good in a bikini Lvarado, I can see why Zac and Harris recommended you for this assignment."

"Thank you Sir." Dana blushed while trying to hide her involuntary smile.

"How much do you know about the operation?"
"Not much Sir, only that it requires a female officer to go undercover in a bathing suit, Sir."

"In other words, Lvarado, nothing Zac, tell her the rest of this so-called plan."

"Of course Captain." Espinoza turned his chair towards Alvarado.

"We have been tracking the Las Casas drug cartel for the past two years now. The leader of the cartel is a Columbian, Jorge Las Casas his top lieutenant is another Columbian, and Arquilio Crespo. We believed that Crespo heads the Las Casas operation in

Florida. He lives in Honduras, but he travels between Las Casas bases throughout the Caribbean. The Las Casas organization is responsible for over seventy-five percent of the cocaine that moves through Miami Dade County. The cartel is also behind at least six murders that we know of including a cop and two informants."

"We have information that on the twenty-third of this month Crespo will be hosting a party on his yacht. That ship will be parked somewhere off the Florida coast where it will be accessible to his guests and his associates."

"Probably just inside the Gulf Stream," Harris interjected "Our intelligence says that's as close to shore as he likes to venture."

"Whatever," Hendricks said "Goon, Espinoza." "As I was saying, at 8:00 am on the twenty-third, a fishing boat will be leaving the Coconut Grove Marina. There will be two crews from Renee's catering on that boat. The first group of eight women and one man will include the serving women and the chef The chef is our informant, He's going to get you on that boat."

"Who's in the other crew?" Lvarado asked.

"Prostitutes," Espinoza answered. "Renee's Catering is really a front for a escort service owned by Las Casas, that's why we can get you in as a server

Renee's has no regular employees, just stringers who work on an as-needed basis. Our man, the chef, will drug one of the serving girls and you'll take her place."

"OK, then what?"

"You'll be carrying a bug and a transmitter. We need you to plant the transmitter somewhere on the deck. It doesn't matter where just somewhere out of sight. Then we need you to plant the bug somewhere inside, either in the main cabin, the conference room, or the entertainment salon. Just get in, plant the bug, and get out. We'll pick you up at the dock when the boat returns."

"Sounds simple enough but just one question why couldn't the chef plant the bug?"

"Crespo's goons will be watching him," Harris answered. "They won't be suspicious of a serving girl in a bikini."

"A bikini?"

"The serving girls will all be wearing bikinis, I mean very small bikinis, actually do you have a problem with that?"

"Um, no, but where will I take my weapon?"
"Thank you Alvarado," Hendricks interrupted

"Go ahead, Espinoza, tell her this part."

"You won't be carrying a weapon or a radio or a phone."

"That's why I hate this fucking plan detectives."

Hendricks shook his head "She won't be able to carry a goddamned weapon and she can't fucking contact us."

"The chef will have a gun packed in his supplies," Alexander said. "If a situation develops, you can go to the galley and retrieve it, and you can always talk into the bug."

"Do you hear that, Alvarado?" Hendricks asked,

"You can go to the galley and retrieve a weapon that's beautiful. What I want to know is, what if she can't get to that fucking galley?"

"Can I ask a question?"

"Go ahead, Alvarado," Hendricks answered. "Why are we handling this operation? Why not

turn this over to the Feds?"

"The Feds don't care about Crespo." Zac

slammed his files on Hendricks' desk.

"They're after Las Casass as far as they're concerned, Crespo can shit all over this county and we get to wipe his ass. They don't care about our murders -not even our dead cop."

"Is that why we aren't working with them?"

"Damn straight Crespo's going to answer for taking out Detective Trujillo."

"I see, 1'min I'll do it."

"Are you out of your fucking mind?" Hendricks bellowed "No, we're not doing it. Its off, you're dismissed, Alvarado, Espinoza and Harris, I want a word with you both."

Cadet Alvarado stood up and headed for the door. She reached for the handle and pulled.

"Alvarado," Hendricks called "I'm expecting big things from you, don't let me down."

"Yes Sir," Alvarado answered. Blushing, she stepped through the door way and closed the door behind her.

"That girl has balls," Hendricks remarked. "I can see why you thought she's capable of pulling this off."

"Sir, this will be Crespo's first visit to this jurisdiction since last April," Zac said." If we let him go, it could be years until we get another shot at him. The Feds aren't going to help us, we owe it to Trujillo's widow."

"Don't play the grieving widow card, Espinoza."

"He was my partner, damn it, and I promised Yolanda we would catch his killers."

"We will, Espinoza, in due time" Hendricks said. "Sir," Harris said. "Will you think about it, at least?"

"I'll take it under advisement. Now get out of here, I have works to do."

"Yes, Sir."

The two detectives stuffed their loose papers into files and headed for the door.

"Espinoza," Hendricks said without looking up from his computer screen.

"Yes?"

"Give my best to Yolanda." "Yes, Sir."

"Now get out of here."

Zac and Harris filed out of the Captain's office. Three nights later Harris and Zac met at their favorite rendezvous. Candee's Espinoza liked Candee's because the eight foot high wall of concrete block surrounding the parking lot afforded a measure of privacy, the lighting inside the club was almost non-existent, and the music was so loud that there were no chance of his conversations being overheard. Over years of patronage, Zac also managed to develop relationships with some of the dancers, who whispered rumours into his ear while he stuffed twenty dollar bills into their garter belts and panties.

Espinoza ordered a draft beer for Harris and a double scotch on the rocks for himself after the waitress returned with the drinks. Zac nudged Harris and pointed to his ear. Alexander turned looked at Espinoza and leaned in his direction.

"I think Crespo may be moving his party up a week," Espinoza said.

"Did the chef tell you that?"

"I haven't spoken to him yet." "Then how do you know?" "Little Kitty let it slip."

"Is Crespo stocking his party with Candee's strippers?" Harris asked.

"No the entertainment is still coming from Renee's, as far as I know."

"Then what does she know?"

"Jackson, the owner, was supposed to be gone all day on the twenty-third and twenty-fourth. He's changed his plans now it's the sixteenth and seventeenth."

"So?"

"He's on the guest list for Crespo's party."

"I see," said Harris "Why didn't the chef say anything?"

"I don't know, but I'll find out when we get out of here."

"Damn, if that's true then we only have ten days to get everything in place."

Two women wearing only bras and g-strings approached the table. Espinoza grabbed the taller of the two, a slender African-American woman who called herself "Black Diamond. The shorter woman, a buxom blonde who went by the name "Precious" settled onto Harris' lap Espinoza slipped a twenty into the woman's garter belt before his roaming hands explored the woman's dark, glitter-covered skin.

Harris slipped a ten into the blonde's g-string and then buried his face in her neck.

"Hey, Alexander," Espinoza called over the woman's shoulder "Is your girlfriend still on board?" "Of course,"Alexander answered without looking up. "Without her, we wouldn't have anything to discuss."

Espinoza kissed a trail from Black Diamond's collar bone to her breast. He swallowed her small orb, and then bit down on her nipple. The dark woman gasped "Stop that," she cooed in an unconvincing manner why should I stop? You say that like it's a bad thing "You know you're going to make me cum" "So."

"It is if other guys see you doing that, they'll think they can get away with it, too."

Zac released the nipple, but then kissed his way to her other breast and repeated the procedure Black

Diamond ground her crotch on his thigh and gasped. "Enough," she said "You have to stop." Espinoza released the nipple and looked over his shoulder at Harris, whose face was buried between the busty blonde's breasts while his hands were kneading her naked buttocks, her g-string sat in a crumpled heap on the table.

"Alexander," Espinoza called.

"Not now, I'm busy," a muffled voice responded, "I just wanted to say, that was a pretty convincing

performance Dana put on in front of the Captain."

"She's good, We can count on her."

"Make sure she's available if that date is really moved up a week."

"Don't worry - Dana's all in she'll make it workout, "I'm counting on her, she's the key."

"Relax she's on board, she knows how much this operation means to me. This is my best chance all year to earn that Sergeant's badge if we can bring Crespo, it's promotion time."

"You better hope so, Harris if you don't make it this year, one of those up and comers like Sullivan or Taylor is going to bypass you."

"I'm well aware of my situation, you don't need to remind me."

Harris slipped a long dark finger between the blonde's legs and rubbed it against her slit. Within seconds his fingertip was glistening with her juice. The blonde shook her head from side-to-side, but Alexander ignored her admonition. She tried to back away, but Alexander's held her in place with a his strong right arm. After several seconds he removed his finger, held it to the his nose, and then held it in front of the dancer's mouth. Her tongue flicked out and licked the finger. She smiled and then leaned forward and kissed him.

"Watch out," Espinoza teased Harris "If Precious

gets hold of that black dick, she might not let go." "You'd best be worrying about your own shit,"

Harris answered "I'm handling my business, by the way, are you still banging Yolanda?"

"Twice a week. Where do you think I'm going after I talk to the chef?"

"I don't blame you, keep it wet, my friend keep it wet."

Zac turned onto Yolanda Trujillo's street a little after midnight. The security light came on as soon as he pulled his car into the driveway. The garage door opened as he shut off the engine, He got out of the car and entered the house through the opened garage; which closed behind him as soon as he enters.

The house was so dark, a soft hand took his and

pulled him into the kitchen, as soon, as he was inside he, was enveloped in a tight embrace by a curvy woman in a silk negligee, she looked up and kissed him, pushing her tongue into the back of his mouth. "I wasn't expecting you tonight Carlos," Yolanda whispered "And I don't think you were expecting me, either."

"Why do you say that?"

"Because you smell like a whore," she answered. "Cheapper fume, discount make up, and coconut oil lotion - you've been to the strip club, and some island girl was rubbing her body all over you. I used to smell that on Ivan all the time."

"I'm going to smell like you when I leave."

"Oh, so you think so Detective Espinoza?"

"I'm going to have your scent all over me, from head to toe—starting with my face."

Espinoza kissed Yolanda on the neck and then continued lower, past her breasts, down her belly and to her crotch. He pulled her panties to the floor and buried his face in her pussy.

"Let's go to the bedroom, Carlos I don't want the kids to see us."

"Right behind you."

An hour later, Zac got up and grabbed his clothes. "Is that it? You only came over here to fuck me, and now you're leaving already?" Yolanda sat up in the bed.

"You know I can't stay." "Of course, Your wife?"

"Once the divorce is final I'll be able to do whatever I want, but until then, I have to sleep in my own bed."

"You can fuck in my bed, but you have to sleep in your own bed? That doesn't make any fucking sense."

"She's—difficult and her lawyer is a real cunt, She wants my balls mounted in her trophy case."

"So tell me, Carlos, was that the only reason you came over tonight? Just to tear up my pussy? Or do you have something for me?"

"Well, Yolanda, I was going to wait until it's final. But since you asked, yes I do have something. We're putting together an operation to go after Crespo but I can't tell you the details, but within two weeks or a month at the most, we should have enough to put him away for life--maybe even get him an appointment with Ole Sparky."

"That's a wonderful news, but Carlos why didn't you mention it before now?"

"We're still working out. It has to go through channels, you know."

"I wish you would have told me that earlier, I would have probably let you put it in my ass after hearing that news."

"I guess I should have led with that."

"Come back to bed Carlos, I think I feel like celebrating." "Yolanda. I can't."

"Where would you rather be? Here, fucking my tight round ass, or home with that bitch of a wife who want to castrate you?"

"I can't stay."

"I see. OK Go ahead, go home and I'll take care of the my situation myself, I can go on the internet I'm sure it won't be too hard to find some big strong man who wants to come over here and shove his hard cock up my tight little asshole, I'll be fine then. Good night, Carlos."

"Yolanda."

"Make sure you lock the door on your way out."
"OK, you win get out the lube."

"I think I'm out, get my lotion off the counter in the bathroom and don't keep me waiting."

"I'll be back before you're even in position"
"Please hurry I'm so fucking horny."

Three days later, Alvarado met Harris and Espinoza at a little Jamaican restaurant in North Miami. Espinoza ordered food from the counter while Harris grabbed four Red Stripe lagers and two ginger beers from the self-service cooler. Alvarado set up the booth with napkins and plastic ware, Alexander handed the two ginger beers to Alvarado, and set the Red Stripes between himself and then Espinoza was the last one to return to the booth. He was carrying a plastic cafeteria tray loaded down with curry goat, jerk pork, meat patties, pea's and rice, and coco bread.

"Don't keep us waiting, coño," Alexander chided Espinoza "What did the Captain say?"

"He said it's ago," Zac answered "We're on." Alvarado distributed the food when she was done, Espinoza and Harris had huge piles of the savory meat and rice on their plates, while hers contained a single meat patty.

"Is that all you're eating?" Alexander asked,

"If I'm going to be on a boat all day wearing a bikini around all those beautiful women, then I'm not touching any of that," Alvarado answered, pointing to the mounds of food on the men's plates "Infact, I shouldn't even be eating this."

"Relax baby," Harris said as he spooned some of his food onto her plate. "I'm sure none of those sluts looks any hotter than you and besides, it's still a week away you've got plenty of time to lose the weight."

"You don't know what it's like if I'm carrying even one extra pound, those bitches will talk, they'll point fingers and giggle every time I walk by and then I'll get pissed off and throw one of them overboard, and that'll blow my cover."

"Just stay alert, keep your eyes open and your mouth shut if anything goes wrong, we're going to have a hard time getting you out of there."

"What do you mean, 'if anything goes wrong?' I thought you said nothing would go wrong?" "Dana, things can always go wrong," Espinoza answered "We planed for that."

"All of a sudden I'm feeling a little less confident about this operation because I thought the two of you have all the details worked out."

"We do, baby, we do," Alexander said "But there are always variables that we cannot control." "Hold on! Stop I don't think I want to do it" "Dana, we won't let anything happen to you." "Do you trust me baby?"Harris asked.

"Yes."

"We'll take care of you," Zac said.

"It's just that I'll be out there all alone."

"Once you activate the bug, we'll be able to monitor everything and we'll have you covered don't worry" Espinoza set down his empty beer bottle.

"Baby, I promise. We'll be minutes away nothing will happen, I would never let anything happen to you.I " know you wouldn't, I know OK I'm sorry. I don't know what came over me I was just....

I'm so sorry."

"It's OK I understand Carlos, can you give us a minute?"

"Sure."

Carlos opened his second beer and walked outside for a second. "What is it, Dana?"

"I'm better, I just panicked for a second. I'm not really trained for this, and you know."

"You impressed the Captain, he wouldn't have approved this operation if he didn't think you could do it."

"You're right I only have three more weeks, and

then I'll be an official member of the Miami PD. I'm as ready as I'm ever going to be, I guess."

"Are we good now?"

"Yes go get Carlos" "I'll be right back" "I love you"

"I love you too, Dana."

Carlos and Dana arrived at Levan's apartment at exactly 5:00 am on Saturday morning, Dana poured coffee while Carlos and Levan spread out the Crespo file in the living room. Dana passed mugs to Carlos and

Levan, and then set hers on the coffee table. She

dumped three teaspoons of sugar into her cup topped it off with half and half, and then sat on the floor with her back to an old lounge chair.

"Hand me those photos, Dana," Carlos said,

Dana picked up the photos that were stacked next to her feet and handed them to Carlos, She then returned to her previous position with her back against the chair and her feet spread wide, her legs splayed at a ninety-degree angle.

"Pay attention, everyone, "Carlos said "We only have an hour to go over everything."

"We've been over the entire operation, and I don't know how many times already," Dana protested "I can recite Carlos' entire speech in my sleep."

Dana leaned to her left, folding her torso over her extended leg. She held that position for five seconds, straightened her torso, and then repeated the movement with her right leg.

"Dana," Levan barked "This is important."

"I'm sorry I'm a little edgy this morning Stretching helps me relax."

"We don't have time," Levan pleaded.

"I said I'm sorry OK? Continue."

Carlos held up a photograph of a scruffy male in his mid-thirties with unkempt black hair and a bushy moustache.

"This is Julio, AKA 'the Chef' He's your contact, Don't speak to him look at him or in any way, acknowledge him unless he speaks to you first understand?"

"Yes."

"There can't be any indication to anyone that the two of you know each other."

"Understood."

Carlos held up a photograph of a well-dressed older man with blonde hair styled in a very bad comb-over.

"This is Bryan Jackson He owns strip clubs all over South Florida. We suspect that he's helping Crespo launder Las Casas' money through his clubs. If he's there, then this party, is the real deal, keep your ears open if you see him. Pay attention to whomever he's talking to."

"Yes, Sir."

Carlos held up a photograph of a stocky black man with a shaved head, a goatee and a mustache.

"This is Franklin Davis He's Crespo's electronics

specialist, Do not let him see you planting the bug or the transmitter. Don't let anyone see you, but most especially don't let him see you."

"Gotcha."

Carlos held up the last photograph, It depicted a Latin male with short dark hair, dark eyes, a black mustache and a goatee.

"This is Crespo Do not approach him under any circumstance Stay as far from him as possible. He's a cop killer He'll kill you if he finds out you're a cop"

"Well, then it's a good thingI'm not yet," Dana responded,

"You better be taking this seriously, Dana" Levan stared into her hazel eyes "These are dangerous men."

"Relax, baby, I'm serious" She turned to Carlos and pointed at the last photograph in the folder "Who's that?"

"That's Trujillo," Espinoza answered, "Ivan Trujillo, my former partner, he was killed while trying to infiltrate Crespo's organisation."

Dana took the photograph and stared at it. A young, handsome, face framed by black hair stared back at her. The teeth were dazzling white and movie star straight, but it was the brilliance of the icy blue eyes that froze her in place.

"He was a handsome man," Dana finally mumbled "His wife must really miss him."

Harris suppressed a chuckle as Zac snatched the photo from Dana's grasp.

"I'm sure she does," Espinoza said after a long pause "I'm sure she does."

Carlos set down the photos and picked up a large tube with a shoulder strap. He opened the end of the tube, pulled out two sheets of paper, and spread them out on the floor.

"This is the layout of the yacht "Carlos pointed to the sheet on his left "The first thing you must do is that find an exterior metal surface that is not easily visible. The upper side of the transmitter is magnetic. The undersides of this fighting chairs should work fine". Carlos circled two fighting chairs at the back of the boat. "Otherwise, this ladder here, or this railing". Carlos circled twoother points on the diagram. "I don't like the ladder or the railing as much, but you'll have to use whichever one you can get to without being spotted. If you choose the ladder, it has to be a rung below eye level."

"Gotcha."

"Here's the transmitter" Carlos handed her a plastic capsule approximately one and half inches long and one inch in diameter "Open the capsule, take out the transmitter, twist it to the right to turn it on, and then attach it to the metal surface. Throw the plastic capsule overboard."

"How long is the battery good for?" "Four hundred hours."

"Cool."

"Next, proceed to the lower level. This is the main cabin, this is the entertainment salon, and this is the conference room". Carlos pointed to three rooms on the diagram. "This is the listening-device"Carlos handed her a green plastic capsule. "Open the capsule, remove the bug, and turn this dial to the right then. Place it under a table, under a shelf, in a light fixture-- anywhere that it will not be detected. It has an adhesive surface that will stick to any smooth surface. Once you've planted the bug, go back to the party and serve drinks until it's over. Renee's boat will bring you back. We'll be in the parking lot of the marina to pick you up."

"And during the party?"

"We'll be in a fishing boat less than a mile away," Carlos answered,

"Don't worry baby, we'll be there if anything goes wrong," Levan added.

Carlos handed Dana a shopping bag. "Here's your uniform."

Dana opened the bag and pulled out a tiny yellow bikini.

"Size eight? What the fuck?"

"I thought the last time your blue" Levan stumbled.

"Do I look fat to you? I wear a six, jackass." "I'm sorry."

"This is all I'm supposed to wear all day?"

"Chef says that's what all the serving girls will be wearing," Carlos said, "just be thankful you're not one of the entertainment girls."

"Why's that?"

"They don't even get the bikini" Carlos laughed

"Do you mean--?"

"Yep Nude totally nude all day."

"I'll take the bikini but just one question: How do I carry these capsules before it's time to use them?"

"Harris, do you want to take this one?"

"Uh, sure" Levan turned to Dana "Baby, I think you realise there's really only one way you're going to be able to smuggle these capsules on board, right?"

"I was afraid you were going to say that."

"I'm sorry."

"That's alright just the next time I'm expected to carry contraband of an electronic nature in my pussy, could you make sure it vibrates, at least?"

Dana arrived at the Coconut Grove Marina at ten minutes to six then. She located a white Dodge delivery van parked near a tree and pulled into the empty space on the passenger side, she locked her car and entered the van.

"Good morning," she said, "I'm Dana."

"No, you're Lydia got that? Lydia" dark haired man with a bushy moustache and tattoos up and down both arms addressed her.

"Lydia."

"That's right "Lydia Zapata Lydia Zapata" "Don't you forget, if anyone asks, you're Lydia

Zapata."

"Got it Lydia Zapata and you're the chef?" "Name's Julio, but everyone calls me 'Chef' "Nice to meet you, Chef I'm Da Lydia. Who is Lydia, by the way?"

"That's the bitch sleeping in that Toyota over by the entrance, I got her drunk last night and gave her some Ambien so she won't be waking up for a couple of hours. Espinoza will call her in before that, and she'll end up spending the weekend at the Krome Detention Center ICE. Will have her back in Guatemala by Monday night. So this weekend, you're Lydia."

"One more thing."

"We don't have time for one more thing. Time for you to get your pretty little ass over to dock eight. The other girls should be there already, and I'll be there as soon as I get my supplies unloaded. Don't talk to anyone unless they talk to you first and don't talk to me at all."

Dana started to answer, but Chef held a finger to his lips and pointed at the door handle, Dana nodded her head, got out of the car and headed for the boat.

It was a short walk to the dock nineteen, young women were gathered in front of a ship where a Thirty-Seven foot Sea Ray was being prepared for departure. Seven of the girls wore yellow bikinis similar to the one Dana was wearing. The other twelve were dressed in various shorts, skirts, and tank tops all the women were between eighteen and twenty-five years of age, slim, tanned, and gorgeous.

Five minutes later Chef arrived at the dock pulling a cart loaded with large coolers and supplies. The two men helped him unload the cart and stow the supplies in the main cabin. Once all the supplies were on board, they began helping the women onto the boat, Most of the girls crowded into the cabin, but there was not enough space for all of them, Dana found a seat at the stern against the transom. She was joined by two of the colorfully dressed girls who she immediately recognised as prostitutes.

When the boat finally departed around 7:30 am, most of the girls had dozed off. The sudden revving of the engines woke all but the hardiest sleepers. The boat trolled out of the marina and into the channel marked by tall buoys on either side just outside of Stiltsville, the operator opened up the engines as he left the bay for the open ocean. He turned toward the southeast and proceeded at full throttle.

At 9:00 am the operator eased up on the engines, Dana looked up and saw that they were approaching a floating behemoth that more resembled a space ship than any water craft she had ever seen before.

The boat was at least one hundred and twenty feet of sharp angles and streamlined surfaces; it was colored a shiny metallic grey and there was smoked glass everywhere. The array of electronic dishes and antennae on the top of the ship looked like a communications satellite that fell out of orbit and embedded itself on the roof. It stood out like a gleaming, foreboding gem amid the sparkling blue of the ocean and the bright morning sky.

The crew of the Sea Ray threw bumpers over the port side of the boat as the captain maneuvered it into position alongside the yacht. A ladder was lowered from the deck of the yacht to the waterline. The crew helped the girls climb from the ladder up to the main deck. Once they were all safely boarded, the crew loaded the supplies onto a net that was hoisted onto the boat.

The first thing that Dana learned when she boarded the yacht was that the diagram of the ship's layout Espinoza showed her was all wrong. This yacht had three levels rather than two, and the outdoor decks were too small for a party of the size that Espinoza and Harris described. For the first time, she started to wonder if her participation in the mission was even a good idea.

The twelve entertainers were taken to the third level. Dana and the other seven serving girls were led to the ship's galley by Chef, they were assigned various tasks but for the most part they spent the rest of the morning setting up for the party and assisting with food preparation. The ship's conference room, the dining salon, and two lounges were rearranged to accommodate the guests, a DJ unloaded and set up his equipment in the conference room, as at 1:00 pm the preparations were completed, and the girls were told they had an hour to eat a little and freshen up before the first guests were expected to arrive.

Dana attempted to use her free hour to explore

the yacht. She didn't get far, an armed guard stood at the stairway junction leading to the first and third floors. The sleeping cabins, which were all located on the first level, were off-limits Likewise, the main entertainment salon on the third level was also out of reach. The conference room, a dining salon, two lounges, the galley, a changing room, and a map room comprised the only level she was able to investigate.

A little before 2:00 pm, the first guests arrived. Brightly painted cigarette boat pulled up to the yacht; two men and two women climbed the ladder and boarded. The Cigarette sped away just as fifty-seven foot. Hatteras eased up to the stern. Eight passengers were transferred to the yacht. The Hatteras departed and an older but pristine Donzi took its place, leaving three passengers on board.

Over the next two hours, a steady stream of yachts and go-fast boats pulled up to the ship, dropped off their passengers, and departed. Most of the guests were directed to the conference room. Occasionally, Dana noticed certain male guests were escorted to the upstairs entertainment salon.

The serving girls were divided into two groups then four of the girls were assigned the task of serving drinks. The other four were expected to carry trays of canapes, hors d'oeuvres, and various other treats prepared by Chef out of the kitchen.

Dana grabbed a silver food tray so that she would not look out of place venturing in and.

When the party first got under way, it was easy for Dana to maneuver with her tray throughout the second level rooms. But as the afternoon wore on then more and more guests arrived, the spacious yacht started to feel cramped. With no prior experience in the food service industry, Dana was surprised to find out that the only time she could move without incumbrance was when her tray was empty. Moving through the crowd while the tray was loaded required all of her concentration. As a result, she did not notice when Bryan Jackson pulled up in a gleaming Cigarette and was quickly escorted to the third level salon.

Starting at 6:00 pm, the serving girls were given rotating half hour breaks. One drink server and one food server were to take their breaks at the same time, followed one-half hour later by the next pair.

Dana drew the final pairing, which meant she was required to remain on her feet until 7:30 pm.

When her break finally arrived, Dana headed straight for the outer deck. The small space at the stern was occupied by guests taking a smoking break, so she walked around the cabin to the front of the ship. Then she found a metal rail where she could attach the transmitter, but the dark windows looking out at her position made her nervous. She walked more around the deck until she found a spot where there were no windows and no guests.

Dana looked to her left and right, she squatted to the deck, reached between her thighs, and pulled the first capsule from her bikini. She opened it, removed the transmitter, and twisted it into the 'on' position. Looking to her left and right again, she tossed the capsule overboard, and then spotted a metal surface next to a large darkened window. The window made her uneasy, so she walked around the deck again.

Two circuits later, Dana realized she was running out of time. She didn't have a watch on her, but she guessed there were less than ten minutes left before she was to be expected back in the galley. Dana looked around to make sure no one was watching her, and then stuck the transmitter to the underside of a railing just a few feet from another of those ominous black windows.

Dana made her way through the crowd and headed for the stairway. Seeing the armed guard blocking her access to both the up and down stairs, she turned into the conference room, then she went over some options in her head, and realized that none of the locations Espinoza specified were accessible. The cabins and the entertainment salon were off-limits. The conference room was fully occupied, her mission was a bust!!!

Frustrated, Dana returned to her station, she stopped in the galley, picked up a tray, and resume serving the guests. There were still six hours before the party was expected to wind down, six hours to come up with a way to get to either the first or the third decks.

A little after 10:00 pm, Dana was returning to the galley with an empty tray when she heard the unmistakable sound of someone getting sick in the ship's head, she set down her tray and knocked on the door but there was no response, a minute later she heard another round of vomiting and then a flush then. She decided to get help but didn't know who to call Chef? What could he do? Another server? crew member?

Just as she was stepping away, the knob turned and the door cracked open. Curious, Dana peaked inside, a naked blonde girl was kneeling in front of the toilet, her face buried inside the bowl, Dana stepped inside, locked the door, and knelt next to the blonde. Dana scooped up her hair and held it away from her face while the next surge of vomit rushed out of her mouth.

When she was through emptying her stomach into the toilet, the naked woman looked up at Dana. Her face was red, her make up was smeared, and trails of black mascara were streaming down both cheeks. Her eyes were bloodshot and her lips were cracked dried, semen was crusted in her hair and between her thighs. She smelles like sex, marijuana, alcohol and vomit "Thank you," she whispered.

Dana filled a disposable cup with water and handed it to the girl.

"Are you alright?" Dana asked,

"I'll just oh fuck!" The girl turned her head toward the toilet as a dry heave wracked her body "I can't I can't go I can't do it" the girls robbed "I want to go home."

"I'm afraid that's not an option." Dana stroked her arms and back. "You're stuck here for at least four more hours."

"No I'm oh god, I can't go back up there."

"Is it that bad?"

"I'm too wasted, Those men there's so many of them I just want to go home."

"I have an idea but first, let's get you cleaned up."

Dana wet a towel and washed the girl's face, she wiped the semen and vomit from her chest and thighs, and then rinsed off her pussy. When she was done, she took off her bikini and put it on the blonde.

"Go to the galley tell the chef you're filling in for Lydia, you're going to have to carry a tray of food around for the rest of the night, but at least you won't have to go back up to whatever hell you came from. Can you do it?"

"Yes," she nodded "I was a waitress before I became a whore."

"Why do you do it?"

"Money, mostly and the drugs are better." "Alright give me a minute to get ready, and then get to work."

Dana opened cabinets and looked through drawers, pulling out whatever she could find and setting it on the marble counter-top. She managed to locate an eyeliner, two lipsticks, and an almost empty bottle of a foundation. She also found a can of hair spray and a brush. So she quickly applied a coat of foundation, and then added a excessive amount of eyeliner before finishing with the lipstick. She teased her hair up and out, and then doused it with hair spray to preserve the volume. She looked in the mirror, added another coat of eyeliner, and then turned to the blonde girl.

"Time to get back to work Remember, you're now Lydia Got it?"

'Yes."

"Good, now get going."

Dana opened the door, directed the blonde toward the galley, and then turned in the other direction, she strutted up to the guard stationed at the stairway. The guard didn't even flinch when the beautiful woman grabbed his crotch and whispered in his ear.

"Are they going to let you boys come up for a while?" Dana pressed her nude body against the guard's chest.

"Not likely," the guard grumbled.

"Too bad, I've been waiting all day for some real cock to show up, You feeling me?"

"Maybe next time this party's for all the VIPs."

"I think you're a VIP," she cooed.

Dana kissed the guard on the cheek, squeezed his cock, and headed up the stairs.

The first thing Dana noticed when her trembling hand opened the door to the main entertainment salon was the thick cloud of cigar and marijuana smoke that hung in the air and seemed to cling to every surface of the room. The lower level party guests all stepped outside to light their cigarettes, cigars, and various illegal products. The stern deck-- including the jacuzzi and the area around it--was the designated smoking area for the hundred or so people celebrating on the lower floors. The VIPs did not practice the same courtesy.

Slipping inside the salon, Dana eased along the

wall in search of a surface where she could plant the listening device. Looking around the room, she was surprised to find out that most of the guests and the whores were not engaged in sex. One blonde girl with tattoos covering both arms and most of her back was on her knees while a large, muscular man with a huge cock was holding her head in his hands and forcing his shaft into her throat, what a pig. Streams of drool were running out of her mouth and down her chest, while mascarastained tears were streaking her cheeks. Despite her distress, the girl was not complaining as she did her best to accommodate the massive rod.

An older, slightly paunchy blonde-haired man was reclining on a sofa while a gorgeous, busty black woman with long braids was riding his cock. The man was pinching the girl' s nipples in a savage manner. The girl responded by lifting her ass up and down at a faster rate every time he increased the pressure, and slower when the pressure dissipated. Another pig,

Dana recalled the photos from her briefing and identified the man as Jackson, the club owner.

Off to the side Dana saw four boisterous men playing cards on a low wooden table surrounded by large leather recliners. The men were all naked, as were the four women entertaining them. One was kneeling on the floor blowing the dealer; the other three were seated on the men's laps.

Another twelve to fifteen men in various states of undress and the other five nude women were scattered around the room lazing on furniture, drinking, doing drugs, or shouting taunts at one another. There was a bar at the far end of the salon where two of the men were shouting and poking each other in the chest. The bartender handed the men their drinks and then they walked away laughing. Strangely--I can't still find anyone who resembles Davis or Crespo.

Along the back wall, a row of tables held various delicacies, the guests had been consuming all day. The first table contained trays of cheese, assorted breads and crackers, cut fruit, and berries while the next table held a black-hoofed Spanish ham on the bone, grilled lamb chops, various cuts of grilled beef, pork, and sausages of all types. The last table was loaded with ice sculptures carved into female bodies, The sculptures contained stone crab claws, cagier, jumbo shrimp, oysters, clams, then assorted sushi and sashimi.

Distracted by the food, Dana's growling stomach reminded her that she had not eaten since one in the afternoon. During her evening break, she was so busy trying to complete her mission that she skipped dinner. At that moment the delicacies arrayed before her eyes--and stomach--were just too tempting.

Dana grabbed a piece of cheese--manchego--and ate it with a cracker. She popped a luscious, ripe strawberry into her mouth, and then moved to the next table. She grabbed a small sausage and found it a little too spicy for her liking. She sliced off a piece of the ham, and then made her way to the last table where she picked up a shrimp and then headed for the sushi.

"Have you tried the fugu?" a voice asked her stunned, Dana turned around and saw a very handsome man with bronze skin and shoulder length black hair standing behind her, he was wearing only a pair of gauzy white pants that were almost transparent. His body was lean but muscular--not bad for someone who appeared to be in his mid forties xcept for the hair on his scalp, he was completely shaven, sizeable cock and heavy balls formed a generous lump in his crotch. Looking at him, Dana felt her face flush as goose pimples erupted on her arms. She knew without looking that her nipples were sticking out like pencil erasers.

"The what?" she managed to ask after a long pause.

"The fugu--Japanese puffer fish properly prepared, it's the best tasting fish in any ocean."

"And if prepared improperly?" Dana asked,

"It's poisonous literally, there's no known anti dote."

"Why would anyone eat it then?"

"Like many things in life, with great risk comes great reward. Are you a risk taker? I'm sorry, I'm afraid I didn't catch your name."

"Lydia, I'm Lydia Lydia Zapata and no, I'm not a risk taker."

"That's funny, you impress me as someone who takes great risks, and who is accustomed to earning tremendous rewards, Lydia Zapata."

"You must have me confused with someone else"
"Perhaps you know, it's funny, I don't remember

seeing you here all day."

Dana's heart almost stopped convincing story. "One of the other girls got sick, her first instinct was to lie, but she did not have time to compose as

I was sent up here to take her place."

"That's unfortunate, I hope the poor girl isn't suffering too badly. But in a way, I'm glad to hear that I don't know how I could have missed seeing someone of your exotic beauty. I thought either my eyes were going bad or my memory was failing. I can't tell you what a relief it is to know that there is a perfectly logical explanation for your presence here "Now."

The man leaned forward and put his arm around Dana, pulling her body against his naked torso. He bent down and touched his lips to hers Dana's dry mouth opened instinctively. She felt his tongue flicker against her lips, she opened her mouth wider and accepted the stranger's probing. Her knees went weak for a second, her face flushed, and she felt her pussy becoming moist. The stranger slid his hand to her butt cheek and squeezed before breaking the kiss.

"I-I think I'll try the fugu," she said in a gasping voice.

"You won't be disappointed, I promise you."

The man used a pair of chopsticks to pick up a slice of the raw fish. He held it to Dana's mouth, she looked at the delicate filet, looked into his liquid brown eyes, and looked back at the fish. She closed her eyes and opened her mouth. The man set the sliced fish on her tongue and withdrew the chopsticks, Dana closed her mouth as an explosion of flavour danced on her palate. She savored the taste for a second, and then chewed and swallowed.

"Wow," she blurted "That was amazing. That's better than sex."

"That all depends," the man responded with a grin "Depends on what?"

"Not what—whom, it all depends upon with whom one is having sex I'm sure that sex with you will be better than any food one could possibly consume."

Dana's face froze she recalled that she was almost a cop posing as a prostitute on a boat filled with dangerous drug dealers, she was no longer gliding under the radar. Her false bravado got her into this mess and she didn't have a clue how she was going to get out of it.

"You're too kind," Dana stammered, "Flattery will get you everywhere."

"Oh, Lydia," the man smiled, "there are so many places I want to go with you."

"We'll visit all of those places, Señor. Do you mind if I try a little more of the fugu, first?"

"Eat as much as you like, beautiful lady. When you've finished, get yourself a drink and then come join me."

"I'll just be a moment; I promise, "Don't keep me waiting too long" You've whetted my appetite."

The man flashed a wolfish grin before turning and walking away.

Dana reached for another piece of fugu, but her fear rendered the fish tasteless, she stopped at the bar and asked the bartender for a shot of tequila. She drained the glass as soon as he set it on the black granite counter. She asked for second shot and then a third. By that time the first shot had reached her brain and she decided she had stalled long enough, she set the glass down and scanned the room for her suitor.

It only took a second to find him, he was seated on a long leather sofa with a stunning brunette seated to his left. The woman was nuzzling his neck while he drank from a large brandy snifter. The man lowered his glass and fixed his gaze on Dana. I'm being summoned.

Dana sauntered over to the sofa. The man whistled his approval as he patted the space to his right. The golden-skinned brunette did not even look up. As Dana sat on the sofa. Dana saw her legs fidget for a second, and then noticed that the man's left hand was buried in her crotch.

"Lydia! What a surprise!"

"Are you busy?" Dana asked "I can come back" "Not at all" The man removed his hand from the brunette "Please, sit with me."

"Lydia, have you met" The man turned to the brunette, "What's your name again?"

"Yazmin," the brunette answered "Yazmin? Of course Lydia, have you met Yazmin?" "Um, no."

"Lydia, Yazmin. Yazmin, Lydia."

"Uh, hello," Lydia said Yazmin rolled her head and looked up. Despite displaying bleary, bloodshot eyes, Dana could see that she was a smoldering beauty with a mop of jet black hair; skin several shades darker than her own, long, shapely legs, and an ample bosom.

"Hello, Lydia," Yazmin purred "are you going to play with us?"

"I have a little bit of business to attend to at the moment," the man interrupted "Why don't the two of you get acquainted until I get back?"

"Uh, sure," Lydia answered "Take your time."

"I'll only be a minute Yazmin will see that you're comfortable until I get back."

The man stood up picked up his glass, and stepped away Yazmin looked at Dana and smiled

"You're hot," Yazmin slurred,

"You're wasted," Dana answered "Kiss me" Yazmin leaned into Dana. Dana pulled back, but Yazmin fell into her "Stop moving," she mumbled, "I think you need to sober up a little," Dana said as she tried to peel Yazmin off her.

"You know what I think? I think you've never been with a girl before."

"I think I'm not going to have this conversation with you right now. We'll talk about that when you're sober."

"Are you trying to get us both killed?" Yazmin whispered, "He wants to see us together."

Dana realised she was in way too far over her head. The simple operation that was reviewed in her boyfriend's apartment had blown up; she had no choice but to ride out the explosion--and hope that she survived the shockwave. She took a deep breath, closed her eyes, and leaned into Yazmin.

Yazmin brushed her mouth against Dana's protruding lower lip, Dana stiffened upon the contact but returned the kiss after a brief hesitation. "This is really your first time, isn't it?" Yazmin asked "Yes," Dana answered. Her body was trembling and her upper lip was quivering.

"Just follow my lead," Yazmin whispered in her ear while stroking her arm "I'll take care of you trust me."

Realizing that she had no choice but to play along.

Dana backed up and looked into Yazmin's big brown eyes. She wasn't sure if she could trust her or how much genuine help she could provide, but a quick review of her situation convinced her that one weak ally was still better than none at all.

"OK," she whispered "Let's do it."

Yazmin smiled and slid her body closer to Dana, pushing her backward into the sofa. Dana shifted to her right, easing her neck and back into the soft leather cushions and then shifting her hips towards

Yazmin. The busty, raven-haired woman took the lead, crawling over Dana and planting her hands in the cushions on either side of Dana. Her full breasts were hanging like ripe fruits, her thick nipples brushing against the rigid pebbles capping Dana's firm, champagne coupe mounds Yazmin looked into Dana's eyes, but Dana turned her eyes to the side. Yazmin lowered her lips to Dana's, commencing a long, lingering kiss that everyone in the room noticed.

Dana stiffened at the contact but with her head and body pressed into the cushions. There was nowhere for her to retreat, she closed her eyes and returned the kiss, parting her lips to receive Yazmin's probing tongue. The kiss wasn't really that bad though, she grudgingly admitted; in fact, it was better than all but a few times that any man had ever kissed her. She forced herself to extend her tongue but pulled it back at the first contact with Yazmin's teeth. Yazmin backed up and brushed Dana's auburn hair from her forehead, kissed her on both cheeks, and then nuzzled Dana's neck.

The contact of Yazmin's lips on Dana's neck sent a spark to the pleasure centres in her brain. Small moan formed in her throat and escaped her open lips. Yazmin caressed Dana's arms, and then the sides of her body. Between the alcohol and the beautiful woman's advances, Dana's mind was floating and she is unsure of what to do or how to proceed, Dana wrapped her arms around the other woman's back and returned the caresses. Yazmin sucked on Dana's neck until she elicited another moan from her, and then closed her teeth to take a gentle bite of her flesh Dana gasped, but continued stroking Yazmin's back.

"I'm going to make you cum like no man ever has," she whispered in the space just below Dana's ear "Do it," Dana replied.

Yazmin left a trail of kisses down Dana's neck and chest. When she reached her breasts, Yazmin closed her lips and sucked a hard nipple into her mouth. Dana stiffened at the contact.

"Relax, honey," Yazmin cooed "You have to trust me."

"I'm trying."

"Don't try so hard, Just let it happen" "OK."

Yazmin alternated her attention from one breast to the other, she sucked and kissed, tasting and teasing the hard little nuggets as she eased her body between Dana's legs. Dana stiffened for a second, before opening her thighs and allowing the darker woman to settle into place, with her breasts grazing Dana's stomach and her hips holding Dana's knees apart, Yazmin left a trail of kisses from her nipple to her navel.

"Oh," Dana gasped.

Yazmin paused for a second before resuming her southbound journey, by the time her lips reaches Dana's bikini line, Yazmin was kneeling on the floor and pulling Dana to the edge of the sofa, Yazmin pushed open Dana's thighs and kisses all over her hairless mound.

"Oh my god," Dana gasped "This is really happening."

Dana placed the palm of one hand on her heart and gripped a sofa cushion with the other, she squeezes her eyes shut and tilted her head backwards, her breath came in short and quick gasps.

"Trust me, honey I know what I'm doing."

"I do," Dana hissed between clenched teeth "I do trust you."

Yazmin placed the tip of her tongue on Dana's

nether lips and licked downward, she removed her mouth and kissed the inside of Dana's trembling thighs, she kissed her opening, tasting the juices that had collected between her pink lips. Yazmin flattened her tongue and licked between the soft folds of tender flesh, she avoided the nub at the top of the slit, concentrating instead on the glistening petals of Dana's tingling flower.

"Oh," Dana squeaked "That's nice."

Yazmin licked her like no man had ever done before. Her touch was delicate and precise, it was almost as though she had a map diagram of the location of every nerve ending, her lips were like warm velvet, and her tongue carried electrical current that excited the flesh in ways Dana never felt before. Every contact of Yazmin's mouth aroused another part of Dana's pussy.

Dana knew a climax was near, but Yazmin's light touch and deliberate pace kept the orgasm at bay. She had never been more aroused, yet she knew she had a long way to go to reach the pinnacle. Yazmin played her body like a virtuoso musician, teasing the melody up ever higher octaves, Dana didn't know how she wasn't cumming already. Her orgasm had become a moving target.

Floating on a cloud of pleasure, Dana didn't notice Yazmin's finger probing her asshole all she felt was another pleasant tingling sensation that bumped her up another level of ecstacy. Yazmin's finger circled her sphincter several times without penetrating, and then withdrew. Seconds later two fingers penetrated her juicy slit, causing Dana to nearly jump out of the couch.

"Hey, what's this?" Yazmin said,

Yazmin withdrew her fingers, pulling the second plastic capsule out of Dana's vagina.

Dana frozed, her heart raced and her pulse quickened, she looked around to her left and right, searching for a door.

"You are a naughty girl!" Yazmin teased "When did you slip this little bullet vibe inside yourself?" "Um, this afternoon right before the guests started arriving."

"It's not doing anything, How does it work?" "Give me that."

Dana lunged for the capsule, pulling it from Yazmin's grasp.

"The battery's dead," Dana lied "Oh well, the guy at the sex shop said it was disposable. I should have brought another one."

"Or spent a fewmore dollars on a better quality model," Yazmin sneered.

Her heart pounding, Dana stuffed the capsule in the sofa, she pushed it as deep into the crevice between the armrest and the bench as she could reach.

"Now let's get back to business," Dana said as she laid back and pulled Yazmin toward her.

Yazmin pushed Dana's knees back into her chest, opening her crotch for a full-fledged assault, She then attached her mouth to Dana's pussy and sucked.

"Uhm" Dana's grunt was barely audible, "Let yourself go," Yazmin urged.

"Just relax and let yourself go, and I'll take care of you."

"Mmm, that sounds good."

Yazmin licked and sucked Dana's pussy lips, swallowing all her sweet juices as though they were water in the desert. Dana's face got hot as she pinched her nipple and squeezed the sofa cushion. She didn't know how much longer she could maintain this balance on the precipice of her orgasm, but she knew what she needed to get off it.

"Lick it," Dana growled. "Lick my clit that was all Yazmin needed to hear", she flattened her tongue and made one last pass across Dana's flowing vagina, and then refocused his attention on Dana's throbbing clit she licked it up and down and then side by side, she sucked it between her lips and squeezed it between her tongue and her upper teeth.

Dana spread her arms wide to grab the sofa cushions arched her back, and exploded. "Uhm ... uhm ... uhm ... uhm."

Dana twisted and strained her body against the soft leather cushions, her arms thrashed and smacked the back of the sofa, but very little noise escaped her lips. It was almost as though she was trying to keep it all inside.

"Uhm ... uhm ... uhm ... uhm."

Yazmin continued sucking on Dana's clit, while Dana continued soaring high and higher on a wave of pleasure. Her senses overloaded she grabbed a fistful of Yazmin's hair and jerked her face from her crotch.

"Enough! I can't take it any more." "Did you like it?"

"Yes! Are you kidding me? Of course, I liked it." "Good, now do you think you can do that to me?"

"I'm not a lesbian, Yazmin" "Neither am I."

"But..."

"It's a skill anyone can do it." "I've never been with a woman." "And now you have."

"But I don't think I can, you know, go down." "Lydia, he's expecting you to do it, I wouldn't disappoint him one way or the other, he always gets what he wants."

"Who is he?"

"That's the boss, this is his boat, his food, his alcohol, his drugs, and we're his girls" That's Crespo? He looks at least ten years older than the pictures I saw "I understand."

"Good, now trade places with me."

Yazmin reclined on the sofa as Dana took her place on the floor. Dana pushed Yazmin's knees apart and slid her cheek against the other woman's smooth thigh. She closed her eyes and extended her tongue to lick the area just above Yazmin's wet slit kiss first? "I'm sorry," Dana blushed.

"I thought we were past that" a girl still likes to be kissed, you know?

Dana stood up, placed one knee on the edge of the sofa between Yazmin's thighs, and leaned into the brunette, Yazmin slipped her hands around the back of Dana's head and pulled her into a tight embrace. Their lips met and Yazmin pushed her tongue to the back of Dana's throat. The tongue retreated as she pulled Dana's head backward.

"Kiss me like you mean it" Yazmin snarled" Kiss me like I'm the lover you've waited for all your life to embrace."

Her head swimming on a sea of alcohol and unfamiliar emotions, Dana leaned into Yazmin and lowered her mouth to the brunette's moist lips, her tongue slithered past Yazmin's teeth and tickled the roof of her mouth. She snaked her tongue as far into the other woman's mouth as she could extend it. Then Yazmin's tongue slipped into her mouth, Dana sucked it with more enthusiasm than she expected.

Once again, Yazmin broke the kiss by pulling back on Dana's hair "What do I taste like?" Yazmin asked "Me," Dana answered.

"What about you? What part of you?" "My pussy.

"Say it, what do I taste like?" "You taste like my pussy."

"That's second hand pussy, are you ready for your first taste of real pussy, direct from the source?"

"Yes."

"Lick me rookie, make me cum."

Dana moved down Yazmin's body, pausing for a second to suck on each of the thick nipples capping her full breasts. Yazmin's hands pushing on the top of her head convinced Dana that she wasn't in the mood for breast play. Dana slid to the floor, parted Yazmin's juicy lips, and started licking.

"That's it, honey," Jasmine cooed "Just lick me like you like to be licked."

Well, here goes nothing. Dana took a deep breath, eased forward, and placed her mouth on the other woman's pussy, she sucked her flesh until it swelled in her mouth. The lighting was too dim to see with any definition, but based on the other woman's black hair, darker skin, and brown nipples, Dana imagined Yazmin's inner lips were dark grey or purple in contrast to her own pink tones.

Dana licked up and down, inside and out, fast and slow, but Yazmin did not seem to be responding. Frustrated, she looked up and saw that Yazmin was taking a hit off a joint, which she then passed to a man standing behind the sofa. That man took an enormous hit, held it until he started to cough, and then passed it to a second man standing to his right, the second man took a hit and then passed it back to Yazmin.

Yazmin looked down and saw Dana staring back at her.

"Oh, I'm sorry, honey take a hit" Yazmin held the joint in front of Dana.

"Uh, no thanks I'm good."

"Go ahead It's OK. This weed is amazing and I don't know where he gets it, but it's the best I've ever had. That's one of the perks of this job, you know-- really, really good drugs."

Dana's training told her to say "no," but she feared creating any kind of disturbance that would tip off the host or his guests.

"Sure, if it's that good, I'll take one hit."

Dana pursed her lips as Yazmin held the joint in front of her mouth, she inhaled quickly and exhaled even quicker, hoping that none of the smoke would find its way past her lungs and into her bloodstream. She lowered her head as the lights in the room seemed to get dimmer, the music became more intense, and then the gravity of her predicament dissipated. She looked up and saw that the joint was still in front of her face (or was it there again?), so she took a second hit.

"Lick it" Yazmin gave Dana a gentle push on the back of her head "Lick my pussy."

Dana shook her head from side to side, her mouth was inches from the gaping pussy of a spread-legged woman, she didn't know. She lifted her head and looked around the room. Where am I? She saw various naked men and women drinking, smoking, and some were even having sex, I'm naked too. The music was loud, and the voices were even louder. She looked up at the breasts of the woman with the splayed legs, she looked past her nipples and into her face Yolanda? Yesenia? Yazmin! Her Name is Yazmin!

Despite the fog pushing down on her brain, everything came back to her in that instant, the boat, the party, Crespo, Yazmin. I had sex with a woman, no- I'm actually having sex with another woman.

She looked again at Yazmin, and then buried her face in the reclining woman's crotch. She wasn't sure why she was licking her, but she felt a small comfort in making love with the only person whose face she recognized. She made me cum I have to do the same for her. Did I say that out loud? Or did I just think it?

Dana glanced upward and saw Yazmin smiling at her.

"Stop looking at me," Dana said
"Why? you're beautiful."

"You're embarrassing me you know, I've never done this before."

"Stop worrying--you're doing fine just follow my lead."

Dana felt Yazmin's hands on the back of her head, guiding her tongue to the exact spot where she wanted to be licked. Dana extended her tongue and slurped the sweet nectar flowing from Yazmin's slit, and then turned her attention to the woman's clit. She squeezed it between her lips, and then introduced it to the tip of her tongue. She flicked the little purple bean with her own pink appendage, stimulating it in the same manner as how she used her finger on herself. She felt Yazmin's fingers crawling across her scalp, pushing with the tips and pulling her hair in fistfuls.

"That's it," Yazmin purred "Oooh, you're getting the hang of it now."

Dana continued licking. Yazmin reached behind her knees and pulled her legs all the way back, affording Dana unimpeded access to her tingling slit. Dana slipped her hands under Yazmin's butt cheeks and lifted her crotch off the sofa. Yazmin arched her back and pressed her clit against Dana's mouth, with every second the friction between Dana's tongue and Yazmin's clit seemed to double.

"Ummhmmm. Ummhmmm. Just like that

You're doing it, wow! Honey you're doing it." Encouraged by her new friend's responses, Dana slipped a finger into Yazmin's slit "UmmmmOooohUhhuh."

Dana slipped a second finger alongside the first, Yazmin started thrashing against her mouth. Dana slid a third finger insider her and then a fourth and she started to wonder how to work her thumb alongside the four fingers before Yazmin erupted.

"Mmmmmm. Uhn! Mmmmmm! Uhn! Mmmmmmm! Uhn! Mmmmmmm!"

Her body thrashing on the sofa, Yazmin's four long moans were punctuated by three strong grunts, and then she collapsed against the cushions.

"No more please, Stop, You did it, Stop."

Yazmin pushed Dana's face from her crotch, and then pulled her up into a tight embrace.

The room erupted in applause. Dana looked up and saw over a dozen men circling the sofa, some of which were hard, some were soft while some were in the process of being coaxed to erection by a naked girl either sucking or stroking their manhood.

"Kiss me," Yazmin whispered in Dana's ear.

"You were wonderful though."

Dana lowered her lips to Yazmin and brushed her lips against the trembling woman's mouth,

"Now you taste like me" Yazmin smiled.

"So I do," Dana blushed,

"Am I not delicious?" Yazmin giggled,

"No more so than me," Dana purred.

"I'll settle this matter" a male voice interrupted Dana's revelry.

Dana looked up and saw the boss's handsome face hovering over her, the glass of cognac in one hand and a fat cigar in the other. His cock was still flaccid, but the bulge in his pants seemed to be longer, thicker, and more pronounced than when she last saw it.

"Come with me, Lydia."

It sounded more like a command than an invitation, Dana hesitated for only a second before taking the proffered hand and following him to the center of the room.

"Have a seat," he said.

The only place for her to sit was the cocktail table where the four men were playing cards. Dana sat on the edge of the table, her presence disrupted the game, but three of the men did not seem to mind though. The fourth man threw down his cards and stared off at distance. Dana crossed her legs and folded her arms in front of her chest. She looked away from the leering men who seemed to have forgotten the naked companions sitting on their laps.

The shirtless man returned with two tall shot glasses and a bottle of Tequila. He set the glasses on the table and poured, he handed one glass to Dana and lifted the other in his right hand.

"To an evening of exotic beauty, immense pleasures, and unexpected gifts Salúd!"

"Salúd" Dana clinked her glass against his, and swallowed the Tequila in one gulp "It's good, right?" he asked "Very good," Dana replied without smiling, "This is an ultra añejo, It's aged over three years."

"Interesting."

"You know, I own the distillery where this is made."

"Really?"

"Well, not entirely though, I am a fifty-one percent owner. My new accountant has diversified my investments.

Spreading the risk, he calls it I now have my fingers in more businesses than I can keep track of. I have money flowing in from parts of the world that I never even knew existed, I don't know how he does it, the man is a complete genius."

"Is your accountant here?"

"Unfortunately, no, he is taking care of a rather distasteful personal matter for me that can not be avoided."

"That's too bad, I would have loved to meet this genius of yours."

"Yes, you impress me as a woman who would be interested in a certain kind of man." "What kind of man is that?"

"Successful men, talented men, men of power, men with refined tastes, men who appreciate objects of rare beauty."

"This genius of yours, he is such a man?"

"To an extent, he works for me, you understand." "Of course," Dana said "and you are such a man?" "Definitely." "I'm impressed."

"One more?" The boss picked up the bottle of Tequila "Uh, sure."

The dark handsome man refilled the glasses with the rich amber liquid. "To men of power, and their beautiful women."

"To men of power," Dana responded.

Dana drained her glass and set on the table. No sooner had she set it down that he was refilling it.

"To the women they adore," he said.

"Two women," Dana slurred "Me and Yazmin." Dana drained her glass and then set it on the table. She lifted her hand to her chest, but in doing so, she knocked the shot glass over. It rolled off the table and fell to the floor. Dana leaned over to pick up the glass when she sat up, the host's pants were open and his cock was hanging in her face.

"What's this?" she asked.

"You know what this is, my lovely little whore." "If we're going to do this, can we go somewhere a little more private?"

"We could, yes, but why would I deprive my guests of your surpassing beauty? Am I not a generous host?"

"Of course you are, Señor, but I could do things for you in private that I would never do in public" "anything we could do in my stateroom we can do here as well and I assure you, we will do those things, all of them."

"But ..." "Enough talk."

The boss placed a strong hand on the back of her head and pushed her face to his crotch. Despite the haze clouding her mental functions. Dana recognized her cue to perform, she opened her mouth and accepted the thickening shaft that was dangling in front of her. She cupped the owner's balls as the stiffening cock swelled in her mouth. In seconds it was fully erect; long, thick, and rigid, it stretched her jaws and poked the back off her throat.

Dana closed her eyes to block out her awareness of the other men and women in the room. She wrapped her free hand around the base of the shaft and licked the head like an ice cream cone. She squeezed his balls and stroked the shaft, using her own saliva as lubricant.

"You have a natural talent for sucking dick, Lydia, you don't suck like a whore."

Removing the shaft from her mouth, Dana paused before responding.

"It's something I enjoy doing, I get a lot of practice."

The man stepped out of the pants that had fallen to his ankles. Holding Dana's head in both hands, he bent over and pressed his lips against her mouth. This kiss was more urgent than the first one they shared. Dana felt her nipples stiffen as the man's tongue slithered over hers, she parted her lips to accept more of it as he explored the inside of her mouth. It was several seconds before she realised her tongue was fully extended into his, as well as strong hand pinched her right nipple, sending a jolt of electricity to her swollen clit. Dana knew she was about to get fucked, and there was nothing she could do to stop it. Apart of her feeling guilty for not trying to get away, but another part was totally ready for it to happen.

Breaking the kiss, the man eased her down onto the wooden table. He then spread her legs and pushed them backward, two hands grasped her ankles and pulled them apart. Only my gynaecologist has ever seen me this open, the man lowered his body over hers, his rigid manhood dangled and waved over her hungry pussy like an angry viper seeking prey. Dana reached for his cock and directed the head against her opening. The man pushed, spreading her lips open as the mushroom head stretched her widening channel. He paused, withdrew, and then pushed again, his second thrust opened her further. He withdrew and then pushed again, burying the last inch of his cock inside her, he's almost as big as Levan.

The man pulled out and then pushed in again, he supported his upper body with his arms, but allowed enough weight to press down onto Dana's torso so that she would completely pinned against the table. Not that she was thinking of going anywhere, anyway best to let the older, handsome, and very dangerous stranger use her for his pleasure. She was more likely to live long enough to catch the boat back to shore if she pleasured him than if she angered him. There's nothing to gain by getting myself killed.

Thrusting in and out of her, the man, settled into a deliberate rhythm. On the up stroke, he slowly drew his cock out so that only the tip would still be inside her. He paused for several seconds, and then thrust downward with enough strength to force an involuntary grunt from Dana's throat. He followed with two very quick strokes before slowly withdrawing once again.

Dana gasped when she felt the man's lips on her neck, followed a second later by his teeth. He gave her several gentle bites on both sides of her throat before moving to her mouth. When he pressed his lips on hers, Dana responded by shoving her tongue as far into his mouth as it would go, a wave of heat flashed over her body as her hunger rose and threatened to devour her. The shame and guilt she felt earlier were being pushed to side as the regimented pace of the man's thick, long cock thrusting in and out which ignited her pussy like never before. The wide head and fat shaft alternately teased and then stabbed her slick tunnel, displacing her organs as it pushed and pulled her closer to an explosion.

"Cum for me," the man implored.

His breath on her neck and his voice in her ear nudged her another notch toward her destination. She was oblivious to her surroundings, her fingernails were embedded in the man's back. In the distance she heard a woman's loud moans overpowering the music emanating from the speakers, it wasn't until the moans became screams that she realised they were her own.

The man abandoned the deliberate two-speed rhythm, replacing it with a steady regimen of long, hard, forceful strokes. His tongue was buried in her throat as he pushed in and out of her with increasing speed.

"UmmUmmm! Ummm! Ungh!" Her moans filled the room.

"Cum for me," he demanded,

"Umm! Ungh! Ummmm! Ungh! Oooooooooo! Ummmmm!"

"That's it, Lydia That's it Cum! Cum!"

"Ungh! Ummmmm! Ahhhhhhh!"

Dana felt like she was melting, sizzling wave of pleasure exploded in her brain, setting every nerves ending on fire, she dug her nails deeper into the man's back and thrashed on the table. The men holding her ankles lost their grip, she kicked one in the face, while the other jumped out of the way of her churning legs.

By the time she stopped writhing, Dana was ready to curl up in a ball and fall asleep. She opened her eyes and saw the man standing over her his cock was still erect.

"Didn't you cum?" she asked.

"Not yet, no."

"But I thought what happened?"

"No problem, my lovely lady I am a man who savors life's pleasures. Tonight I'm enjoying your magnificent body so much that I do not want the pleasure to end."

"So you --just stopped?"

"A short break, that is all. Now that you have caught your breath, we can continue"

"Umm, can I rest a little, first?"

"Lovely, lovely Lydia, you are without question the most beautiful whore I have ever enjoyed, but you are still a whore--a whore who is working for me. I don't know who trained you, but the first thing you should have learned is that the word 'no' is not part of your vocabulary, and it is something you can never, ever, say to me."

Dana's jaw dropped. The colour drained from her face, her lip quivered, and a tear rolled down her cheek.

"I'm sorry," she managed to utter after several panicked seconds.

"How can I please you?"

"Turn over on your hands and knees."

Dana hurried into the position, The men and women surrounding the table backed up to give her some space. The hardwood surface was rough on her knees and elbows, but she thought better off protesting.

"Not there, on the floor."

Dana scrambled to the deck, the carpet felt softer than the table, but she knew that she would wake up in the morning with rug burns. She dreaded the thought of explaining them to Levan.

"Put your face down all the way." Dana lowered her face to the carpet. "Spread your butt cheeks."

Dana reached back took a cheek in each hand, and pulled them apart.

"Lovely Such a lovely sight, Lydia I could admire you all night."

The man stood up and walked away, Lydia tried to follow his feet, but he stepped out of her limited field of vision. She considered running, but she knew there was nowhere to go. Fleeing, she decided that was the worst thing she could do.

The man returned a minute later, he poured liquid all over her crotch, she couldn't see what it was, but the odour of it somewhat resembled olive oil. The man stood over her with his feet on either side of her hips. He bent at the knees, lowering his still-erect cock to her crotch; He slid his cock up and down her slit and all along the crack of her ass. When his cock was as slick as her crotch, he placed the tip against her asshole and pushed.

"Not there! that's the wrong hole!"

The man said nothing instead, he continued to burrow Dana's hands reflexively shot back and pushed against the man's torso. Two men grabbed her wrists and pushed them up and into the centre of her back.

Pain shot through her shoulders, She considered kicking her legs, but she realized that her arms would be dislocated or broken before her legs found a target, she was immobilised.

"Please," she protested. "Not there you're too big."

Dana knew from experience that the man's cock was too big once after a night of drinking, she tried to take Levan's cock in her ass, he couldn't even get the head past her sphincter. It was the first and only time she had ever attempted anal sex until now.

"Stop!" Dana sobbed "I don't like it in my ass!" The man continued pushing pain shot through her torso, starting in her rectum and ending in her stomach, then different kind of pain rippled through her shoulders.

"Just relax, Lydia this doesn't have to be painful."

Dana knew she was helpless. Resistance was only going to get her hurt or killed in one way or another, he was going to get in her ass. The only question was how much damage she suffered before he finished. Because fighting is pointless.

"OK OK Just give me a second"

The man relented. He didn't back up, but he stopped moving forward.

Dana took several deep breaths.

"Tell these men to let go of my arms."

The two men looked up at him. He nodded and then let go of her wrists.

Dana took several more deep breaths and willed herself to relax.

"OK," she said,

A burning pain tore through her guts as the man resumed pushing. Despite the pain, Dana resisted the urge to squeeze. She felt her sphincter yielding as the fat head pushed its way into her rectum.

"Unnnnnnnnngh! Oh god, that hurts!" Dana cried.

Dana felt as though she were being ripped in two. Her ass was on fire while a stabbing, nauseating sensation was shredding her bowels. She tried to breathe, but the pain was shutting down her bodily functions. Just as she was about to pass out, she felt a spike followed by a sudden lessening, the man stopped pushing.

"The worse is over," he said "The head is in"

Dana felt like she had been penetrated by a jagged metal crown encrusted with jewels. Her ass was still burning, but the searing pain in her gut was gone. Her ability to breathe returned back. She took several deep breaths and then braced for the next wave.

The man resumed pushing, his cock penetrated her ass inch by inch. When it was halfway in, he pulled back and poured more oil on his shaft then he set the oil down and pushed again. Fresh wave of hurt washed over Dana, but it was less intense as inch after inch of thick cock filled her ass, Dana became accustomed to it. After several minutes, of slow penetration interrupted by brief withdrawals, Dana felt his balls slapping against her pussy lips the man paused.

"Are you alright?"

"I'm coping," she answered.

The man started pumping in and out of her tight little butthole.

"Go slow," she pleaded.

The man grabbed her hips and pushed slowly at first, he then thrust his cock in and out, pumping faster as every minute elapsed.

"Gentle this is my first time."

Dana reached between her legs and flicked her clit. The fire in her ass never went away, but she thought if she could rub herself to an orgasm then that sensation might overwhelm the pain. In any event, the sooner the man came the sooner her ordeal would come to an end.

"Easy Easy hhh--not so hard."

The man thrust into her at a steady pace, his fat cock stretching her asshole over and over, Dana reached a point where the nausea went away and the burning became manageable I think I can endure this if it doesn't get any worse.

"Like that," she urged "Just like that"

The man was slamming into her butt with controlled but forceful thrusts, Dana felt like her asshole was shredded into confetti. Despite her best efforts, she was no closer to an orgasm than when she started. She doubted that she would ever be able to shit again. Her fingers stopped flicking her clit as she contemplated the rest of her life with a colostomy bag.

"Mmmmmm! Mmmmmmmmm! Mmmmm! Ungh!

"The man grunted. "Here cums! Ungh!"

Dana felt a different kind of warmth in her bowels, the man's pace slowed and his grip on her hips lessened and second later his cock slid out of her ass, followed by a stream of semen.

Overwhelmed by all the Tequila, marijuana, sex and pain, Dana collapsed on the floor.

Espinoza and Harris stood at the end of the dock taking turns looking through the binoculars, It was after 3:00 am. They had just exited their boat and were waiting for the Sea-Ray to arrive. Harris heard the distant engines before he saw the boat's lights. The two men retreated to the parking lot and waited for the passengers to disembark.

Nineteen girls got off the boat, but Dana was not part of them.

The chef followed several minutes later, Alexander and Espinoza were waiting for him at his truck.

"Where's Dana?" Harris shouted,

"I don't know," Chef answered "She didn't get off the boat."

"What the fuck do you mean she's still on the boat?"

"She went upstairs and never came back down" "Chef, you're pissing me off" Espinoza pulled his gun and pressed it against Chef's forehead.

"Tell me where the fuck she is."

"Look, all I know is that around 11:00 am drunk prostitute stumbled into the galley and told me she was replacing Lydia and I never saw your girl again."

"Did you look for her?"

"Hell no, they had armed guards at the stairs and

I wasn't allowed to roam around that boat."

"Why did she have to go upstairs? She should have been able to plant the bug on the main level, What was Crespo doing upstairs?"

"Crespo wasn't there, It wasn't his boat."

"Whose boat was it?" "Las Casas."

"Las Casas? I thought Crespo was hosting the party."

"That's what Renee told me but I don't know when the plan changed."

"Get the fuck out of here Chef and don't say a word about this to anyone."

Chef got in his van and speed off.

"Well, what are you waiting for for?" Harris said to Espinoza "Call this in, We've got to get the Feds to go after them."

"We can't call anyone."

"What do you mean?"

"We don't have any support, this operation was never approved."

"What? you've got to be fucking kidding me but you said Hendricks approved it."

"I lied."

Harris slammed his fist into Espinoza's stomach, Zac doubled over, but Harris hit him in the face with an upper cut then Espinoza fell to the ground, unconscious.

"Dana!"Harris shouted into the early morning sky "Dana!"

CHAPTER 2

Dana awoke with a pounding in her head and a feeling of nausea deep in her stomach, an experience which was no doubt worsened by the gentle but constant rocking of the bed upon which she found herself. She forced her crusted eyelids open but regretted that decision almost as soon as it was made. The light stabbed her retinas through her wide-open pupils, searing the back of her brain with the intensity of a supernova. She snapped her eyes shut and covered her head with the heavy comfort blanketing her aching body.

Where in the hell am I? What happened? Why am I feeling like shit?

Slowly opening her eyelids, Dana stole a glance from beneath the duvet. The stabbing in the back of her brain returned as she focused her vision. The setting was unfamiliar, but the rocking motion revealed all she needed to know.

Fuck! I'm still on the goddamned boat!, and I'm still naked! Where the fuck are Alexander and Espinoza?

Dana crawled out of bed and shuffled across the room to a window, she pulled the curtain to one side and peered out.

We're docked somewhere, but I don't recognise the port. Dana ran through a quick inventory of the various marinas from which she had gone boating ever, it wasn't a longlist Coconut Grove? No Bay- side? Definitely not Black Point? No way Miami Beach? No Fort Lauderdale? I don't think so. The sun was already high in the sky, and her field of vision was populated by old fishing boats and small dinghies. The few pleasure craft she saw were all smaller sized, although there were a few larger sailboats occupying slips off in the distance, then she saw a tall lighthouse attached to an old stone fort overlooking the harbor, I have no idea where the fuck I am.

Dana made her way to the door and checked the handle unlocked, great! She turned the handle, pulled the door open, and peered out into the hallway. She didn't see anyone, so she took one step through the doorway and then changed her mind. She returned to the bed, put her head beneath the covers, and cried.

An hour later there was a knock at the door, Dana poked her head from beneath the blanket and listened.

The knock repeated itself then Dana held her breath and laid motionless. She feared that her pounding heartbeat would give her away, but the door remain closed.

Dana was unable to go back to sleep. Despite her best efforts, she was also unable to formulate any kind of a plan. She knew that she was aboard a private yacht owned by a very dangerous drug kingpin. She was naked, hung over, unarmed, and without any means of communicating with the Miami PD. Also, onboard were an undetermined number of men all armed who worked for the drug lord. She had no idea where she was, but the available evidence suggested that she was no longer in the US Crespo, she would never take the risk of docking in an American port.

Her concentration was broken by another knock on the door. She froze this time, the knock was accompanied by a voice.

"Senorita? are you awake?"

Dana recognized the man's voice, I can't hide beneath these blankets forever.

"Come in," she answered.

The door opened and her host slipped through the door.

"Good afternoon, lovely lady," the dark haired man said "How are you feeling?"

"I've been better."

"I'm not surprised last night you drank nearly an entire bottle of my best Tequila" "This doesn't feel like a mere hangover."

"You don't remember much, do you?"

"I remember you violating my ass."

"Ah, yes that is a memory we both shared, it's one that I will always cherish."

"Cherish' isn't exactly the way I'll look back on it."

"Do you remember much of what followed?" "I'm a little fuzzy on the details."

"You sampled a little of every substance that was offered to you, at least half a dozen of my guests enjoyed your company. In fact, more than one tried to take you home as they departed. You finally passed out around 4 am door."

"No wonder I feel like shit."

That's when I put you to bed in my stateroom and posted a guard outside.

What have I done?

"Unfortunately, we don't have much time for you to recover. I let you sleep as long as I could, but we're expecting guests in an hour. Take a shower and get yourself cleaned up while I have the Chef fix you something to eat and I'll be back in thirty minutes with your food."

"The Chef is still here?" Dana's eyes opened wide, He can get me a phone, at least and he has a gun.

There may be a way out of here" He didn't go back to shore?"

"My personal chef always travels with me. He prepared all the delicacies I served in the VIP room, and some of the food for the lower level, as well, the rest was done by some line cook out of Miami, he packed up and left just before we departed."

Dana's heart sank, a lump formed in her throat, but she forced herself not to cry, I won't - not in front of him.

The man turned to leave.

"Can I ask one more question? "Dana said,

"Ofcourse." "Where are we?" "Marina Heming way." "And that is?"

"I'm sorry Havana Harbor."

"Havana? Cuba?" Dana's jaw dropped, "Ofcourse."

The man walked out of the stateroom, closing the door behind him. Flood of tears streamed down Dana's cheeks. What happened to the surveillance and pursuit? They were supposed to be watching me. Not only am I outside the US, but I'm in a place in North America where there is absolutely no hope of rescue.

Dana took a long hot shower, there was an assortment of soaps and shampoos in highend packaging to choose from, but none of the products were familiar to her. Every surface, fixture and accessory in the shower spoke of luxury and class, but the dim memories of the previous night left her feeling like a filthy whore. No matter how much she scrubbed, she could not cleanse herself of the shame and guilt that stuck to her like raw sewage. How many men did I fuck last night? Will Levan forgive me if I ever see him again?

After ten minutes, Dana shut off the water and

dried herself off, wrapped her hair in a towel, and searched through the cabinets for cosmetics. She found a box of new tooth brushes and a tube of toothpaste. She found some women's deodorant, razors, and several bottles of perfume. In another cabinet, she found a hair dryer, some mouse, and a brush. But she was looking for make-up when the door opened and her host returned.

"Are you ready? The chef prepared a wonderful brunch for you."

Dana existed the bathroom, she managed to look radiant despite her lingering nausea.

"Do you have anything I can wear? I seem to have misplaced my clothes."

"You weren't wearing any, lovely lady." The man smiled and pointed to a closet. "Inside that door to your right is a robe you can use. We found a skirt and tank top in the entertainment salon, but I don't think you really want to wear those, do you?"

Dana opened the closet door and removed a fluffy white robe.

"I'll take this, thank you."

"Very good" The man's smile gleamed "Have a seat."

The host walked over to a small table and pulled back the chair, Dana sat in the seat. He removed the dome from a silver tray revealing a plate of food, a glass of orange juice, and a small cup of coffee.

"Eggs benedict with stone crab, a chocolate croissant, and fresh squeezed orange juice and café con leche, Enjoy."

"Can I have some water, please?"

"Of course, of course. My apologies."

The man departed. Dana poked at her plate, picked up the croissant, and took a bite. She washed it down with a sip from the steaming coffee cup. She tasted the eggs and sipped her juice. The man returned with two bottles of ice cold water.

"Here you are," he said as he set the bottles down on the table "Once again, I apologize."

"Thank you, Señor I'm sorry, I don't recall your Name" The man chuckled.

"Last night you called me El Jefe. I'm Jorge-Jorge Las Casas."

Dana nearly choked on her water Las Casas? I'm so fucked. So fucking fucked.

After a long pause in which Dana recalled every conversation, she had overheard between Harris, Espinoza and Hendricks regarding the drug lord, she asked, "Um, who are you entertaining?"

"I'm glad you asked. We are being honored with a visit from El General Eduardo Torres. He is a senior officer in the Cuban military."

"I see and, to what do you owe this honour?"

"I have business with the Castro regime. El General Torres is the government liaison, his portfolio includes all ports on this side of the island."

"OK, I'm not sure that I follow." Las Casas sighed.

"I maintain friendly relations with the Cuban government. I supply cash and other things of value to certain government officials. In return, I am allowed to travel in their waters and port here whenever necessary. This arrangement allows me to evade the United States Coast Guard, the DE, and the US Navy. They can't follow me here. It is a service that I find extremely valuable whenever I am traveling the Caribbean between North and South America."

"Do you have similar arrangements with any other governments?"

"That, my dear, is none of your business. Now, finish your breakfast the General will be here in few minutes."

"What does that have to do with me?"

"You are my co-host. Now hurry up and get yourself ready."

"What am I supposed to wear? This robe?"

"The robe won't be necessary, the General will prefer you in your natural state."

Dana was unable to speak, she stared at Las Casas with eyes the size of golf balls.

Las Casas escorted Dana to the entertainment salon. Stepping through the doorway. Dana recalled the debauchery of the previous night. She was surprised to see that the room had been cleaned to a pristine state. The odours of alcohol and smoke from the previous night were gone; the furniture was all arranged into cozy conversation areas; every surface was polished to a sparkle. The room was almost unrecognisable from the night before.

Las Casas took Dana's robe and draped it over

the back of a chair. He directed Dana to sit, and then sat himself in the adjacent seat, a few moments later there was a knock on the salon door, then the door opened. An elderly gentleman in a green and red military uniform entered the room. He was followed by two gorgeous young women wearing matching red dresses. The dresses revealed a fair amount of cleavage as well as miles of tanned leg. One woman carried a sealed wooden box while another carried a garment bag.

"El General Torres" Las Casas stood and shook the older man's hand.

"Señor Las Casas, my old friend" The General embraced Las Casas, and then turned toward Dana "and who is your lovely companion?"

"This lovely lady is Lydia Zapata," Las Casas said "She came aboard my boat last night, and chose to accompany me for a while. How could I turn her away?"

"Indeed, I would have questioned your manhood if you had. There are pills for that, you know?"

Both men burst out laughing. Dana blushed, while the women accompanying General Torres, rolled their eyeballs.

The General eyed Dana from head to toe. Dana felt her entire body flush, her nipples became rigid, and goose bumps covered her arms. She caught herself futilely attempting to cover her nudity with her hands, and willed herself to let them drop to her sides. The General reached for Dana's hand, bent at the waist, and planted a gentle kiss on the back of her wrist.

"I am pleased to meet your acquaintance, Lydia" The General's eyes gleamed "Very pleased"

"Thank you, El General," Dana replied,

"Jorge, please allow me to present my companions" The General released Dana's hand and waived his arm in the direction of the two women flanking him" These are the Velez sisters, this sweet thing is Micaela, and this one is Ana."

The two women bowed their heads in unison. "They are beautiful sisters you say?"

"Twins, actually." "I thought so." "How?"

"Their father abandoned them when they were very small. He left on a raft for Florida. It is believed that the raft capsized, and everyone on board drowned. Few years later, their mother was arrested and convicted of fomenting dissent. It was some nasty business, she is now serving a life sentence in the Western Prison for Women, although I heard that she is very poor health. The girls were fortunate to be taken in by the Minister of Justice, who took pity on them when they were orphaned."

"I see."

"The government put them through college, and then they served four years in the military."

"Impressive! They have done well to overcome their unfortunate circumstances, they must be very grateful to the Minister."

"They are and to El Presidente, as well."

"Of course."

"On behalf of El Presidente Castro, it is my honor to present them to you as a sign of our appreciation for all you have done on behalf of the revolutionary government."

"I don't know what to say, I'm flattered."

"Ana" The General turned in the direction of the girl on his right then she handed him the wooden box "l so, El Presidente sends you a box of Cuba's finest."

The General broke the seals on the box, opened the lid, and presented it to Las Casas.

"Cohibas, they are El Presidente's personal favorite."

"Please give him my thanks. I am honored." "Micaela." The General turned to his left then Micaela handed him the garment bag, which he, in turn, gave to Las Casas. "This is the clothing you asked for, the twins made the selections."

"I'm sure that their taste is exquisite." Las Casas handed the bag to Dana" As much as I enjoyed seeing you nude, there will be occasions when clothing is necessary."

Dana opened the bag and pulled out a dress. She held it up and then checked the tag.

"Eight?" she frowned "I'm a six" Do I look fat? Micaela and Ana exchanged a quick glance and a brief smile, Las Casas glared in Dana's direction, and then walked behind the bar, he returned with a metallic briefcase, which he handed to the General. "And this," he said, "is for El Presidente."

The general opened the brief case, glanced at the stacks of $100 dollar bills neatly bundled inside and then closed it.

"Señor Castro will be most pleased."

"How much time do you have?" Las Casas asked." Will, you be staying for dinner? My chef is preparing black grouper."

"I'm sure it will be magnificent, but I'm afraid that I cannot stay because my presence is required at a cabinet meeting later this afternoon, I can only stay for an hour or so."

"In that case, let's not waste any time, the twins will accompany me to my stateroom Lydia will entertain you here, El General. There will be a guard outside the door. If you need anything, just ask and my man would get it for you."

Dana frozen, She opened her mouth, but no words came out.

"Thank you, Jorge," the General said." You are too kind."

"It's the least I could do for an old friend."

Las Casas extended his hands in the direction of Ana and Micaela. They accepted and walked with him out the door.

Espinoza sat across the table from Harris. His left eye was blackened from the punch Alexander landed the previous night. He bowed his head, made the sign of the cross, and then plunged his spoon into the steaming bowl of plantain soup in front of him. "Are you sure you aren't going to eat?" Zac asked. "Mother fucker, how can you eat at a time like this?" Alexander snarled.

"We'll get her back, I promise, but I'm not going on a hunger strike waiting for her to return. What goodwill that do?"

"Shut the fuck up before, I blacken your other eye, you half-raccoon mother fucker. This is your fault. Now what did your contact in the Coast Guard say?" "They tracked a boat matching the description provided by the chef. They followed it from a few miles off Key Largo to the Florida Straits. They had to call off their pursuit when it entered Cuban territorial waters. It appeared to be headed for Havana." "God damn, Espinoza, we don't have any fucking contacts in Havana!"

"Keep it down, Harris do you want to get us both fired?"

"Right now, I don't give a fuck. We promised Dana we would keep her safe. We told her the risk was minimal. We failed, and that failure could get her killed."

"I promise you that we will get her back. But you're going to have to calm down, or we're both going to see our careers flushed down the toilet. Do you understand me?"

"Fuck off."

Harris stood up and stormed out the door.

The General watched Las Casas and the twins leave, and then turned in the direction of Dana. His eyes narrowed and a thin smile creased his lips.

"It's almost a shame that Señor Las Casas will be dressing you. If you were mine, I would keep you just as you are now. Even without clothing, make-up or jewellery, your beauty exceeds any woman. I have ever encountered in my sixty-nine years. You outshine my precious twins, I see why he treasures you. You are indeed, a rare and exquisite jewel."

"General, you're making me blush. I'm just a poor girl who fell through a rabbit hole and woke up in a strange world I don't understand.

"Oh, sweet lady, even an old man such as myself can see that you are much more than you profess. If I didn't know better, I might even think that you are dangerous."

"Dangerous? Me? I hardly think so."

"There's more to you than meets the eye and what meets the eye is formidably beautiful, but formidable. That is a dangerous combination in any world."

If I can just keep him talking until it's time for him to go.

"I'm flattered that you think so highly of me, El General, but I'm really just a poor serving girl." "Serving girl with the skills of a courtesan, I am told."

Uh oh.

"You've heard of me?"

"Señor Las Casas men all spoke very highly of you. One of them tried to bribe me into switching places with him while your benefactor enjoys the twins. I turned him down, of course. You're something of a legend, already."

Fuck! How many dicks did I suck last night? "Iuh didn't realize I was so um famous." "Show me how you earned your reputation."

The General gently but forcefully pushed Dana to her knees. He unzipped his pants and fished out his cock. It was fully erect and ready for action.

Dana was shocked to see the old man aroused.

His manhood was not particularly long nor thick, but its appearance was no less shocking. Even fully erect the foreskin completely enveloped the head with an inch of sagging skin to spare. It was not the first uncircumcised cock she had ever experienced, but the flap of skin covering it was by far the most extensive she had ever seen. *I think I'm going to puke.*

Resigned to her fate, Dana rolled back the foreskin and was relieved to see that the head otherwise appeared normal. She circled one hand around the shaft, pulling the skin taught. She then reached into the General's underwear with her other hand to retrieve his balls. The fur-covered orbs were hanging almost to his knees, it seemed-gross-old man balls. *Could this day get any worse?*

The General stood at attention while Dana licked the bashful head. *Maybe it's not so bashful. It could be that it would love to come out more often, but it gets lost in all that foreskin.* That thought caused a wave of nausea to rise up from the pit of Dana's stomach down her esophagus. *I'll probably be killed if I puke on him.*

It took all of her willpower to force the bile. *I better get this over with as quickly as* Dana closed her eyes and concentrated on making the General cum. She worked her left hand on the base of his cock while the right hand massaged his balls. She bobbed her head back and forth, varying the speed and pressure as she used every technique she could recall. *Maybe I should give him a reach around? That sends some guys over the top-like Levan. There are others, though, who think its kind of gay and get pissed off. It's probably best if I just keep doing what I'm already doing.*

The General placed his hands on the sides of Dana's head and thrust in and out of her mouth- Within minutes his intensity matched Dana's. He forced his cock to the back of her throat as long streams of drool ran out off her chin and dripped onto the floor. He fucked her face with the ferocity of a prisoner enjoying his first night of freedom after a lengthy incarceration. The General's orgasm approached he became rougher, pulling her hair and snapping her head from side to side. He slapped her, and then pinched her nose shut so that she couldn't breathe.

"That's it, put a Suck on my cock."

The adoring gentleman who had showered her with compliments was gone, replaced by a cruel old man with an unnaturally hard cock and a disdain for whores. He held her hair with one hand and slapped her face with the other while he continued to shove his cock in and out of her mouth.

Without warning, he held Dana's head in both hands and pressed her face against his belly. His cock was entirely engulfed in her mouth when the first spurts of thick semen erupted in the back of her throat. Holding Dana by her hair, the General pumped one blast after another down Dana's gullet. Her gag reflex attempted to expel both the intruding shaft and its creamy issue, but the General's strong grip held her in place, no matter what, just don't puke.

When he was through ejaculating, the General released his grip and relaxed. Dana slumped backwards, resting her butt on her upraised heels. She did- n't have to think about swallowing-the General shot his load directly down her throat. No residue remained in her mouth. At least that's over.

Las Casas popped open a bottle of chilled champagne and poured the sparkling liquid into two crystal flutes. He handed the flutes to the twins, and then poured dark rum into a brandy snifter.

"To many happy voyages," Las Casas said as he tipped his glass toward the twins.

"Many happy voyages," Na and Micaela responded in unison.

The twins lifted their glasses and drained them at once. Las Casas watched them over the rim of his glass as he took a small sip of the aged rum. The girls set down their flutes and then cozied up to Las Casas.

They each took a hand and directed him toward the bed Las Casas offered no resistance.

Las Casas sat on the edge of the bed and pulled Micaela toward him. He reached behind her and unzipped her dress. Micaela wiggled her shoulders, helping the garment to fall to the floor. It formed a small heap around her ankles. Micaela stepped out of the dress, and then leaned her firm body toward Las

Casas. Her pointed brown nipple was inches from his mouth.

"Would you like to taste it, Señor?" Micaela asked, "Of course," Las Casas replied, "but first, take off your shoes."

Micaela bent at the waist and unbuckled her black sandals. She stood up and kicked them off, one at a time.

"Now undress your sister," Las Casas ordered" Starting with her shoes."

The twins exchanged a knowing glance and slight smiles with one another. Micaela stepped over to Na and knelt at her feet. She unbuckled the left sandal and lifted her foot, and Micaela removed the shoe. The two of them then repeated the process with the right foot. Micaela stood and pulled the zipper down Na's back. She then pulled the dress off her sister's shoulders and let it fall to the floor next to her own.

Before Las Casas could say anything, Micaela turned toward Na, put her hands around her back and pulled her sister's body toward her. Micaela cocked her head several degrees, and then pressed her lips to Na's mouth. Na's hands circled her sister's waist before descending a few inches and settling on her round buttocks. The incestuous kiss continued for a full minute before the sisters finally broke it off. Both girls smiled and then turned toward Las Casas, "How shall we entertain you?" Micaela asked.

"Do you want to watch?" Na tilted her head and lifted an eyebrow.

"Or will you be joining us?" smile spread across Micaela's face.

"For now, I will be content to watch," Las Casas answered. He reached for his belt and adjusted his pants.

"Very well," Na said "Watch but make sure you don't blink, you won't want to miss anything."

The twins stood in front of Las Casas and resumed their kiss, Na turned slightly to her right- Micaela ground her crotch almost bare, but for the landing strip above the slit-against her sister's hip Na cupped a firm butt cheek in each hand and pulled Micaela closer. Their tongues danced in each others mouths as they gyrated against one another smooth, caramel-colored back.

Micaela bit her sister's lower lip as she dug her fingernails into Na's. Na raised a knee and rocked her leg against Micaela's dampened crotch. Micaela glanced in Las Casas' direction and moaned.

The twins broke their kiss and climbed onto the bed. Na laid on her back while Micaela crawled on top of her. Micaela planted her arms in the soft duvet on either side of Na's torso. She lowered her chest until her pointed nipples were just touching her sister's identical chocolate-tipped cones. Her long, shiny black hair cascading onto her sister's face.

Micaela leaned forward and brushed her moist lips on Na's neck. This time, it was Na's turn to moan.

Micaela sat up and looked around the room for Las Casas. She found him standing near the door, slowly taking off his clothes. Micaela locked eyes with him. When she was sure he was watching, Micaela sat upright, gathered her hair, and tied it in a knot on top of her head. She spun around, straddled Na's head, and lowered her crotch to her sister's face.

His clothes folded and stacked on a shelf, Las Casas approached the twins with his erect cock in hand. Las Casas stood next to the bed and offered it to the girls. They ignored him Micaela closed her eyes, arched her back, and rocked back and forth on Na's mouth. Na's eyes were closed, but even if opened her field of vision would have been entirely filled by

Micaela's slender butt cheeks and the moist crevice that divided them.

Micaela opened her eyes and turned to Las Casas.

His eyes were narrowed to small slits, his jaw was set, and his back was rigid. He reminded her of a predator taking measure of its prey.

"Do you like watching, Señor?" Micaela purred.

"Not usually," he answered "I prefer to be actively engaged."

Las Casas stroked his erection and edged a step closer to the bed.

"Patience, please My sister's touch is ahhhhhhh-something to be-mmmmmmm-savored" Micaela shuddered as an orgasm rippled through her body.

"Do you enjoy making love with your sister?" Las Casas asked, the look on his face a mixture of curiosity and revulsion.

"What's not to like about it? We are mmmmmmmmmm identical. No one knows my body better than her.

In many ways, making love with her voice trailed off to a whisper Na is like-uhnnnnnn-making love to myself" Micaela arched her back as "Who wouldn't want that?"

"That's an interesting way to justify your perversion."

"You   consider   us-ahhhhhh-perverse?"
"Absolutely."

"Do we disgust you? Do you find us revolting?"
"Not at all, I'm fascinated" her long moan

escaped Micaela's lips. She leaned forward, pushed Na's knees apart, and lowered her mouth to her sister's pussy. Burying her tongue between the wet folds of pink and grey flesh, she licked up and down the full length of Na's slit. Na's body stiffened as her pussy responded to Micaela's practiced touch.

Within minutes, the aroma of female arousal was stimulating Las Casas through his old factory sense. His hand was still attached to the base of his shaft, but he was unable to keep it from moving. He stood and stroked his cock while inches away the identical twins licked each other to orgasm.

Micaela moaned and groaned as each succeeding orgasm eclipsed the one that came before it. Na licked and sucked, her concentration focused on delivering her sister the ultimate joys her own body inched closer and closer to release. Na sucked her sister's clit between her teeth and whipped it with her flickering tongue. Micaela pressed her crotch against Na's mouth and bucked her hips as she exploded in orgasm.

When her sensitive clit could take no more stimulation, Micaela tilted her hips and lifted her crotch from Na's mouth. In that position her pussy was wide open and her asshole was exposed. She buried her face in Na's crotch, attacking her slit with a renewed enthusiasm and commitment to her sister's bliss.

Las Casas knew his restraint would crumble at some point. The two identical goddesses were among the most beautiful women who had ever found their way into his bed. The smells and sounds alone were torture enough. The sight of Micaela's raised ass and her open cunt was too much. He reached between Micaela's legs and inserted a finger into her soaked pussy It slid in without resistance, "Mmmmmmmmmm," Micaela moaned.

Las Casas withdrew his finger, crossed his index and middle fingers, and then reinserted them in Micaela's juicy hole. He wiggled one finger from side to side while he slid the two digits in and out of Micaela's gaping vagina.

Micaela raised her head for a second, located Las Casas, and reached for his cock. She touched the head, smearing the precum on her palm, and then pushed his hand out of the way. She had taken over the business of stroking his erect shaft.

This time it was Las Casas' turn to moan, he continued plunging his fingers in and out of Micaela's slick cunt while she pulled on his rod and licked her sister to an emerging climax. Micaela increased the pressure of her tongue on Na's clit while she stroked Las Casas' shaft with more urgency. Las Casas plunged his fingers in and out of Micaela's cunt, matching the speed and rhythm of her hand on his shaft. The sounds of wet fingers and tongues and sexual organs punctuated the journey to oblivion.

Las Casas reached his climax first. He grunted

twice, and then shot his load on Micaela's back. Five spurts of thick semen erupted from his shaft and landed on Micaela's spine and shoulders, glazing the area between her shoulder blades.

"No more, no more," he panted as he pried Micaela's fingers from his cock.

Scooping the slick cream from Micaela's skin with his free hand, Las Casas rubbed it into the crack of her ass second later his middle finger was penetrating her asshole. He pushed it in all the way to the last knuckle, and then withdrew it. He alternately plunged the middle finger in her asshole and the two fingers of his other hand into her pussy. In less than a minute Micaela exploded.

"Uhhhnnnnn!   Mmmmmmmmmm! Uhnnnnnnnnn!"

Micaela lifted her head from Na's crotch. With her back arched, her butt up in the air, and her eyes squeezed shut, Micaela endured wave after wave of pleasure Las Casas' fingers continued plunging in and out of both holes, driving her further up the ladder of her ascending climax.

"Stop please. That's enough" Micaela slumped on top of Na "My turn, bitch," Na protested "Lick me." Micaela turned her attention to Na. She pulled her legs back, inserted two fingers into her pussy, and sucked her clit into her mouth. Micaela fucked her with a ferocity that Na was not expecting. She flicked her tongue back and forth, faster and faster. Two fingers became three, and then three became four.

"Oh! Shit!" Na screamed.

Micaela plunged her hand in and out of Na's frothing pussy juices flowed from her cunt, soaking the sheets beneath her ass. Micaela plunged into her deeper and deeper, stretching her tight pussy with her thrusting fingers.

"Oh! Yes! I'm ... ungh! Oh! Ungh!"

Micaela pulled out her and buried her tongue between her sister's folds. She licked and sucked on her lips, biting her clit and slurping her juices

"Ungh! OK! OK! No more!"

Micaela ignored her sister's request. She continued licking and sucking Na grabbed her hair and pulled her face from between her legs.

"No more, please no more."

His cock spent, a smiling Las Casas clapped his approval.

"You two are marvelous," he said "Sick, disgusting and perverted, but absolutely marvellous." "Does that mean you want to keep us?" Micaela asked,

"How could I say no?" Las Casas said, "Are you planning to fuck us? Or was that it?" Na inquired,

"Give me a minute, last night was a very long night. I need a little time to recover."

"Don't keep us waiting too long," Micaela said

"We might decide that we don't need you." "Girls, girls, I'm not as young as I used to be, but I can still handle the two of you."

"That's what the Minister used to say," Micaela said.

"Until he couldn't handle us," Na giggled.

"So, what's your story-the rest of the story? How did you end up with General Torres?"

"The Justice Minister and his wife took us in when our parents abandoned us" Micaela said. "We were twelve at the time. It was about two years later when he started visiting us at night first it was just him."

"But after a while his wife joined in, as well," Na continued.

"Na is that when the two of you?" Las Casas asked, "Became lovers? Yes" Micaela looked at Na "The

Minister and his wife liked to watch." "Now I understand." Las Casas looked from Micaela to Na. "When we finished pre-university, we enrolled at the University of Havana," Na said. "We were encouraged to study government, languages, and foreign affairs."

"We never saw the Minister again, even though we lived in the same city," Micaela added" and then you joined the army?" Las Casas asked.

"We weren't given a choice," Micaela answered.

"That's how we ended up with El General

Torres," Na said. "He trained us in the art of espionage."

"You're with the Intelligence Directorate?"

"No," they both answered.

"El General Torres used us for private matters," Na said.

"Mostly to deal with his rivals in the army," Micaela added.

"And the occasional governmental official who poked his head in the wrong direction," Na said. "I see so, why did he bring you here?"

"When El General first recruited us, he promised that we would see the world," Micaela said "But when

Fidel Castro stepped down and his brother Raúl took over, El General Torres influence was greatly diminished. Raúl has his own favorites El General is just a figurehead, now he runs the ports, but not much else. He can't do anything for us, and he no longer has much use for us."

"Don't you provide him companionship?" "Occasionally, but he is old now and does not partake of our company when his wife is around," Micaela answered "He is retiring, and will not be able to support us on his pension."

"He's hoping that you'll take us away" Na smiled "as are we."

Dana wiped the drool from her mouth with the back of her hand. Now what am I supposed to do with this old guy? Who knows how much longer Las Casas will be with the twins? She stood up and headed toward the bar.

"Can I get you drink, El General?"

"Thank you, Dulcita, but no. My time here is limited, and we still have much to do."

"We do? what?"

"I must finish exploring your luscious body. Your oral skills are impressive, but I'm sure that you have more to offer than a blowjob."

"El General," Dana purred, "I'm flattered" With her back to the General, Dana dropped some ice cubes into a crystal tumbler "Surely you won't be here long enough to start another round. Even a man of your considerable stature requires time to reload."

Dana poured rum into the tumbler. She splashed some juice on top of it, and then poked around the bar for a slice of lemon.

"Not this man,"the General responded.

"Oh?"

Dana turned toward the General. Her eyes met his the General nodded as a feral smile spread across his face. Dana glanced downward, and her jaw dropped. How is this old man still hard? I drained him. He shouldn't get another erection for a week.

"The blue pill."

"Excuse me?" Dana asked.

"The blue pill-Viagra. That's how I'm ready to go. I always take one when Señor Las Casas pays us a visit."

"I see."

Dana raised her glass to her lips and sipped.

"My time is limited," the General said "Entertain me Now."

Dana set her drink on the bar and walked over to the General. She reached for his pants, unbuckled his belt, and tried to push them to the floor. The General grabbed his pants and held them up.

"No there," the General said.

Dana tilted her head and looked at him. The General grabbed her by the hair and dragged her to the leather sofa in the middle of the room.

"Here," he said, pushing her into the cushions.

Dana pulled his pants to the floor. She wrapped a hand around his cock and gave it a gentle tug-Damn! He's still rock hard, I hope his heart can handle whatever he's planning to do. I don't need to be accused of murdering the old lech.

Dana laid back on the couch. With her hand wrapped around his cock, she spread her legs and pulled him toward her.

Smack!

The General's hand struck her cheek.

"Oww!" she cried.

"Not like that," put a the General admonished "Only my wife gets to look at my face, whores take it from behind so they can stare into-the ground and contemplate the fate of their lost souls."

Hypocritical, much? Besides, I'm not really a whore. I only play one on TV Dana chuckled under her breath, and then turned over onto her hands and knees.

"Whatever you say, El General."

The General paused to untie his shoes and remove his pants. He stood behind Dana and rubbed the head of his cock against her slit. The General made no effort to get her wet, so she braced for a rough entry. She felt a cool liquid dripping onto the crack of her ass, and then the General's cock pressing against her asshole. It took a moment for the realization to set in.

"No, not there," she protested please, not in my ass.

"Shut up, whore you will satisfy me in all the ways that my frail wife cannot" "I will," she begged, "I'll do anything, but not that please."

"You'll do everything, including that."

The General pushed from the standing position, his leveraged weight readily provided sufficient force to penetrate Dana's ravaged asshole. His slick cock over came her resistance, stopping only when it was completely buried in her rectum searing pain shot through her body. Her asshole felt like it was on fire. "Ungh!" she groaned. "Please" wave of nausea washed over her as she recalled the beating her ass took the night before Las Casas was the first, but others followed at least the General's not as big. If I wasn't so sore, I could probably handle him.

The General pushed her head into the sofa and then commenced drilling his chemically enhanced manhood into her ravaged sphincter. He plunged in and out of her with long, slow strokes of his rigid cock, savoring every sensation along the way.

"Your ass is a delight, I've never experienced anything so wonderful in all of my sixty-nine years. No wonder Las Casas speaks so highly of you."

"Please," Dana whimpered "No more."

"Fortunately for me, at least-you sucked the easy one out already This next one will take much longer to arrive, I'll have to manage the pace to conserve my strength.

Oh, fuck Goddamn it. Dana buried her face in the cushions and sobbed.

"I don't know why you're acting like this," the General teased "at my age, there is no finer pleasure than the firm body of a beautiful young woman. You are giving me a gift that I will remember all of the remaining days of my life."

I hope you die soon, bastard.

Dana tried to disassociate her mind from her body in an effort to block out the pain. She thought of the academy; she thought of her friends and her career; and then she thought of Levan.

Levan would never treat me so brutally, Levan is gentle and loving. Levan would shower me with kisses and caress my skin Levan would honour me and protect me. But he's not protecting me it's his fault I'm in this mess Levan, Zac, and Hendricks-where are they? Why didn't anyone rescue me? How did I end up in Cuba?

The General continued sawing in and out of Dana's bruised and broken rectum. He paused on several occasions to squirt more lube onto his cock, but otherwise maintained his steady pace for over thirty minutes. Dana buried her face and sobbed into the cushions as flames engulfed her raw asshole.

There was a knock at the door, but the General ignored it. The door opened a crack and one of Las Casas' men poked his head in the salon.

"El Jefe will be here in ten minutes," he said.

The General nodded at the man, who then withdrew his head and closed the door. The General increased his pace.

Dana wrapped her arms around the thick leather-covered cushion in an effort to brace herself for the inevitability of the General's final assault. Her hand slid into the gap between the sofa arm and the bench. She felt a hard object wedged into the gap. She wrapped her hand around it as her mind raced. The bug! I forgot about the bug! I have to plant it before Las Casas returns.

"Fuck me!" she demanded through clenched teeth "Fuck my ass! C'mon, give it to me!"

Hurry up and cum, damn it, I'm running out of time.

"Mmm, yes, I knew you would enjoy it, eventually," the General gloated "whore always likes it when a real man takes her and roughs her up a little."

The General grabbed a fistful of her hair and snapped her head backward so that she was looking up at the ceiling. He spit on her face, and then pushed it into the cushions. His pace quickened as he raced to achieve orgasm before Las Casas returned.

"Fuck me! Fuck my ass! Give me that big cock!" "Mmmm, oh yes, puta, take it. Take it, take my cock in your tight little whore ass."

"Fuck my ass! Fuck me like a whore! Fuck it!" "Get ready, whore get ready almost there almost" "Do it Fuck me harder Fuck my ass Fuck my whore ass!" Sell it. I've got to sell it." It's cumming almost it's cumming."

"Fuck it! Fuck it! Make me cum! Fuck me with that big hard cock!"

"Ungh! hhhhhhh! Ungh! Oh, yes! Ungh!"

"Oh, baby Oh, baby That's so good your cock is so good so good Mmmmm" You ass raping old pervert.

Why don't you go home and try fucking your wife like that? Afraid she'll cut off your balls?

The General withdrew his cock and reached for his clothes.

"Don't you want to clean up, first?" Dana asked "Your cock was drilling my asshole almost to my stomach."

"Of course, of course."

"If you look in the cabinet behind the bar, you should find some hand towels mini refrigerator. There might even be some liquid soap back there, as well. There's bottled water in the."

"My dear, you're forgetting just who is the guest and who is the whore" "I'm sorry" Fuck!

Dana stood and walked behind the bar. She located several small towels, a bottle of hand sanitizer, and two bottles of water. She returned to the sofa and handed the General a towel. She set the remaining supplies on the cocktail table.

"Why are you giving me this? I'm not a maid That's your job."

Dana frowned for a second but regained her composure before the General could see her face. She poured water onto one of the hand towels and cleaned his still erect cock. She then squirted some hand sanitizer onto her palm and massaged the length of the General's cock.

"Thank you," he said, "but I don't think we have time for round three."

Thank God for small miracles Dana poured water onto another towel and wiped her pussy and ass. She placed the damp towel on the cushion between her leg and the sofa arm. She watched the General put on his pants and underwear, and waited for him to bend over to tie his shoes. When he sat on a lounge chair with his shoes between his feet, Dana eased her hand beneath the towel and into the sofa. She watched the General bend over. She fished the capsule out of its hiding spot, and covered it with the damp cloth and slid the towel onto her lap and waited. When the General reached for his second shoe, she stuffed the capsule into her pussy. Her hand returned to the cushion just as the General was sitting up in his chair.

"Can I get you anything?" Dana asked.

"Some cold water, please," the General answered "In a glass."

Dana gathered the towels and water bottles and walked behind the bar. She squatted on the floor and removed the capsule from her pussy. She opened it, removed the bug, and returned the capsule to her vagina. Just as she was attaching the adhesive surface of the bug to the underside of a shelf, the door opened. Dana grabbed a bottle of water and stood up, without switching the device to the 'on' position. "El General!" Las Casas' voice boomed "I trust

Lydia has taken good care of you?"

"She is, as you say, a very rare gem. I was most impressed with her skills. In fact, I was so impressed that I would like to make an offer for her."

Dana's heart stopped beating for a second. Her eyes grew wide and a gasp escaped her lips Las Casas chuckled.

"I'm afraid, old friend; that this one is not for sale."

"That's rather ungracious of you, Señor Las Casas. I'm leaving you with my dear sweet twins-as gifts, no less and you will not entertain an offer to sell me your newly acquired whore? She can't be worth that much to you already that would spurn the good faith offer of a dear old friend?"

"I appreciate your generosity, esteemed General.

However, there would be complications if I were to sell Lydia to you. She is an American. She would not adapt well to living on your island, and that would lead to problems at the highest level. Problems would lead to scrutiny, and that is something none of us can afford."

"Jorge, you have left Americans here in the past" "That was different those girls were damaged. They fell through the cracks and were already forgotten long before I made their acquaintance.

This one would be missed."

"My twins will be missed."

"By you, yes, but I suspect that your wife will be pleased when they do not return. The important point is, that no one will be looking for the mind where I am taking them, no one will question their presence. I can't say the same for Lydia. If I were to leave her here, there would be consequences."

"Very well I suspected as much, but I had to ask." Dana breathed a sigh of relief after the General departed, Las Casas led Dana to his stateroom. He opened the garment bag and laid her clothes out on the bed. There were two dresses, two pairs of shorts, a half dozen tops, two skirts, a pair of jeans, and a tailored suit.

"That should be sufficient until we reach our next destination, no?" Las Casas asked.

"That depends where we are going?"

"Barranquilla."

"Colombia?" Dana gulped.

"Of course is there another?"

"I don't know, actually. That's kind of far from home."

"Don't worry I'll take care of you."

"I'm sure you will" Dana closed her eyes and fought back a tear.

"There is one problem," she said.

"Oh?"

"There's no underwear in here no bras, pantieshose."

"Lydia, it's summer time in the tropics who wears underwear? You're lucky, I requested any clothing at all for you."

"Don't get me wrong, I'm grateful for everything you've done I just, you know I don't go Commando." "Commando?"

"Nevermind."

"The twins brought suitcases, If you need anything, check with them."

"Where are they?"

"They will be staying in the next cabin." "Where are you going?"

"I'll be in the communications salon I have some business that needs my attention."

"When are we leaving?"

"We left fifteen minutes ago." "Oh."

"Stay inside until we're out of Cuban waters, one of my men will let you know when it's safe for you to come out."

"Safe?"

"The Cubans are very strict when it comes to immigration matters. I pay for certain privileges, but it is imperative that they are exercised in a discreet manner."

"Gotcha."

"I'll see you at dinner."

Las Casas turned and left the stateroom. Dana waited until the door was closed, and then curled up in the bed and cried herself to sleep. Later in the afternoon, Dana got up from the bed and put on shorts and a tank top. She went next door and knocked, but no one answered. She knocked a second time, but still got no response. She turned the handle and cracked open the door. Peering into the room, she saw four suitcases, clothing and personal items spread all over the bed, but the occupants were missing.

Dana shrugged and headed for the stairs. She reached the second level and went out on to the rear deck. Stepping into the late afternoon sun, she found the twins reclining in the Jacuzzi with a pitcher of Daiquiris.

"La puta!" Micaela shouted"Come and join us"
"I'm not a whore," Dana responded.

"Of course you aren't," Micaela said "Neither are we."

"Men fuck us and leave money behind, but we aren't whores," Na said. "The money just falls out of their pockets."

"And we were going to fuck someone, right?" Micaela smiled at Na.

"Somehow we just end up with the men whose wives don't know how to patch the holes in their clothing." Ana laughed.

"Or how to suck dick" Micaela and Na slapped a high five.

"I'm not ... whatever."

Dana took off her clothes and climbed into the Jacuzzi. She settled into a corner seat facing Micaela. The hot, bubbling water helped ease the stiffness from her joints. She positioned her lower back against a jet and felt the tension drain from her body.

"This is nice," Dana said.

"Hey, sunshine," Micaela splashed water at Dana. "How long have you been whoring?" "I told you, I'm not a whore."

"Then how did you end up in El Jefe's bed? Re you his mistress?" Na asked.

"I'm a waitress I was serving food and drinks at his party the other girl got sick, and I took her place." "So, you're some kind of Cinderella?" Micaela asked" This boat is your floating magic pumpkin?

Las Casas is your handsome prince?"

"Show me your glass slippers," Na teased. "It's nothing like that."

"I'm not buying it," Micaela sneered "Something about you just doesn't add up." "What do you mean?"

"Your story seems too convenient," Micaela said "Lonely little waitress slash whore goes to bed and wakes up to find herself mistress to one of the wealthiest and most powerful men in the world? I don't buy it."

"I don't care what you think" Dana's face was already flushed from the heat and steam, but it felt even warmer as a wave of emotion overcame her. Tears streamed down her cheeks, "I just want to go home."

"Leave her alone" Na glared at Micaela "Can't you see she's scared?" Na eased over to Dana and wrapped her arms around her.

"Don't worry, My sister and I will watch out for you. You'll be safe with us, Isn't that true, Micaela?" "As long as she checks out, she doesn't have anything to worry about from me."

"Micaela," Na said, "We're going to protect her- Right?"

"Of course."

Dana surrendered to Na's embrace, she buried her face in Na's shoulder as a flood of tears poured down her cheeks.

"Everything will be OK," Na stroked Dana's back" Just be strong."

"How come the two of you aren't afraid?"

"Girl, after what we've already been through, this is a fucking vacation. It's like we're on a cruise, or something." Micaela tilted her head back and laughed" El General and before him, the Justice Minister, those are some seriously fucked up old men."

"What did they do to you?"

"It's not so much about what they did to us-although there was enough of that-but more of what they made us do," Na said.

"To each other?"

"To their rivals," Micaela answered.

"And there were plenty of those," Na added. "Why did the General leave you with Las Casas?" "He owed us for everything we did for him,"

Micaela said "It was a sizeable tab."

"He has cancer" Na looked at her sister. "His days are numbered. He was worried about retaliation against us after he's gone."

"Las Casas smuggled us out of the country for him," Micaela said "He gave us a chance for a new life."

"What will you do?"

"We're hoping that once we get to Colombia, Las Casas will make us his body guards." The twins smiled at one another.

"He has plenty of enemies, you know" Micaela glared at Dana.

"We're very highly trained," Na added.

"Hell, we're fucking dangerous" Micaela grinned.

"I'm sure he does" Dana frowned ", and I'm sure you are."

After two days skirting the southern Cuban coast, they spent the next three days in open ocean, where Dana saw nothing but other boats and a variety of marine life. On the sixth day, Dana was taking a walk around the outer deck when she spotted a patch of land in the distance. Excited, she returned to the stateroom she shared with Las Casas. The bed was still unmade and evidence of their morning fuck was still visible as a large wet spot on the lower sheet. Las Casas was sitting on the edge of the bed talking into a cell phone.

"Two hours," he said into the phone," I'll deal with it then."He closed the phone and placed it on a table. "I saw some land," Dana said to Las Casas "re there islands off the coast of Colombia?" "Yes, we are, but you didn't see one of those."

"I'm confused where are we?"

"The island you saw his Roatán We're going to Honduras."

"Honduras? You said we were going to Colombia."

"There's been a change of plans we had to make a detour."

"Why? What happened?'

"Don't worry about it, we'll get to Colombia but first, I have to take care of some business in Roatán." Las Casas reached for the phone and punched in another number.

"Luis," he said crisply, "Where's the accountant?" Tell him toget Franklin and bring all the printouts, wire transfer confirmations, and account statements. That's right, everything keep them busy until I arrive. I can't wait to hear his explanation.

CHAPTER 3

Dana stood on the deck and watched as the land mass grew closer, first it appeared as an emerald green jewel amid a field of blue, but as it filled more of the horizon. Dana saw patches of color breaking up the greenfield of brown and white resolved itself into a massive house with a terracotta roof and a long dock jutting into the water. Several small boats and a large yacht were tied up along the seawalls the dock drew closer, Dana saw several armed men stationed at regular intervals handful of men stood at the centre of the structure.

It took a good twenty minutes for the ship to dock. Men on the boat threw ropes to the men on the dock, and a structure on wheels was rolled into position for disembarkation. Several men boarded, and several others disembarked. Seemingly forgotten, Dana stood at the bow and watched the activity while she waited for instructions.

Las Casas finally emerged with the twins flanking him. Dressed in identical khaki-colored slacks, navy blue t-shirts, dark sunglasses and black boots, and with their black haired pulled back into tight pony tails, the twin's cut imposing figures. They each wore a handgun holstered around the waist, and an automatic assault weapon slung over their shoulders.

Las Casas wore black slacks, a white linen guayabera, and a white fedora with a black band. The bulges in his shirt revealed at least two weapons concealed in his slacks. He carried the box of cigars the General gave him in Havana.

"Lydia," Las Casas called.

"Yes, Sir" Lydia hurried to meet him.

"Stay in my stateroom until I summon you. I will send for you but until then, stay out of sight." "Is it dangerous?"

"The situation here is unstable, it will be safest for you below deck." "What about you?"

"My people should be in control." "Then why can't I go with you?"

"Until I have a chance to assess the situation with my own eyes, I prefer to exercise caution where you are concerned."

"I see."

"Now lock yourself in my stateroom, and don't open the door for anyone but myself or the twins Understand?"

"Yes."

"This shouldn't take long."

Las Casas turned and made his way off the boat, followed by the twins, he was joined by six of the men who were waiting for him on the dock. The six men formed a hexagon around Las Casas, Micaela and Na. They moved together as one, covering the distance from the dock to the house in tight formation.

Dana retreated to the stateroom she shared with Las Casas. She pulled back a curtain and peered through a heavily tinted window. Las Casas, the twins, and the six other men reached the rear entrance of the house. They disappeared into the back entrance, followed by ten more men who seemed to materialise out of the lush tropical vegetation.

An hour later the rear door opened and a single person exited. It was one of the twins, who sprinted toward the dock, weapon in hand. Dana stood by the stateroom door and waited for a knock. It was a long thirty seconds before she heard the rapping of knuckles against the hard-wood door.

"Lydia, you can come out."

Dana unlocked the door and opened it. "He's ready for you, now," Na said. "What's going on in there?"

"Justice."

"What do you mean?"

"You'll see once you get inside Hurry." "I'm right behind you."

The two made their way off the ship. Dana admired the landscaping even as she wilted in the heat and humidity. I thought Miami was hot. This is ridiculous. By the time she reached the rear door, her face was flushed and a sheen of sweat covered her forehead. So much for my hair. I hope there's somewhere on this island I can get some products.

Na led Dana through the kitchen, past a dining room, and into a large room that served as the main entertainment area in the house. Plush furniture filled the room; paintings and statues decorated every wall and empty corner. Las Casas was seated behind a heavy wooden table placed at one end of the room. There was an empty chair to his left- Micaela was standing behind him at least a dozen armed men were standing at attention around the perimeter of the room.

"Lydia," Las Casas' voice boomed from the far end of the room. "I'm so sorry to have kept you waiting. Please forgive me."

Las Casas stood as Lydia walked toward him.

"It's quite alright. I'm not some delicate flower requiring constant care."

"Come and sit beside me."

Las Casa pulled the empty chair from the table Lydia walked around the table and sat. Las Casas returned to his seat as Na took her place next to Micaela.

"Unfortunately, my dear sweet Lydia, there is more to my business than enjoying good food and drink and the wonderful company of a lovely woman. Sometimes, I'm afraid, my work is truly ugly. Business can be filthy, and there are days when the filth must be cleansed. Today is a cleaning day. Today I must deal with a betrayal by someone very close to me, someone I trusted. Someone I loved like family, lump formed in Dana's throat feared that she would pass out.

Beads of sweat appeared on her forehead, she felt light-headed and I'm not ready to die.

"Bring him in." Na left the room. She returned a moment later dragging a bound man with a black bag over his head. She led him to the center of the room and stood him twenty feet from the table-She delivered a hard boot to the back of his knees, forcing him to the floor. Na removed the bag, revealing a battered face that Dana instantly recognized Crespo!

Las Casas reached to his hip, pulled out a 9 mm Glock and set it in on the table with the barrel pointing directly at Crespo.

"Rquilio," Las Casas barked in a tone Dana had never heard before" It has come to my attention that there are certain discrepancies in your accounts."

"Jorge enough of this nonsense, there has to be a mistake. You know that I would never steal from you"

"My friend, I didn't get where I am by making $30 Million mistakes. If you made that kind of a mistake, then what use do I have for you?"

"That's not what I meant.

"Then please, Arquilio, please help me to understand what has happened here."

"Jorge, I honestly do not know what you are talking about. There are no discrepancies, there are no shortfalls. I can account for every dollar that I have collected on your behalf " sheen of sweat appeared on Crespo's forehead" You can go through my files everything is in order."

"I already have" Las Casas paused to tap the face of his cell phone "That's why I'm here" moment later a door opened and a black man with a shaved head entered carrying a lap top and some manila files.

That's Davis, the computer guy. This is probably why he wasn't at the party.

He handed the files to Las Casas and set the laptop on the table next to the gun. Las Casas opened one of the files and pulled out several sheets of paper Davis leaned over Las Casas' shoulder and pointed to various notations on the papers.

"Thank you, Franklin," Las Casas said," I'll let you know if I need anything else."

Davis turned and left the room.

"Arquilio," Las Casas said in a cool, even tone "I have in front of me a spread sheet showing that my revenues for North American shipments are off by $302 million over the first six months of this year the same time. I have wire transfer memos showing the movement of over $6 million from one of my Cayman Island accounts into a numbered Swiss account.

$5 million into a UE account, $83 million into a Hong Kong account, $46 million into a South African corporation, and $2 million into the Ugandan treasury Over $4 million remains unaccounted for. I presume that you must have some cash lying around somewhere. Do you care to explain, or should I just kill you now?"

"Jorge, I don't know what you are talking about."

"The records speak for themselves, Rquilio."

"I-there must be some explanation, give me a few days to look into them."

"Cabržn! there is an explanation! You're fucking stealing from me you filthy piece of shit!" "I haven't stolen from you I swear."

"We'll get to the bottom of this."

Las Casas turned to Micaela and motioned for her to come closer. Micaela bent over, and Las Casas whispered into her ear. She stood, turned toward the door, and departed.

The twin returned a minute later, she was holding a gun to the head of an attractive woman in a silk dress whose hands were tied behind her back. The woman's bleached blonde hair hung limply to her shoulders. Her eyes were puffy, her make-up was streaked, and tears stained her face. She appeared to be around thirty years of age.

"Jorge!" Crespo shouted "This is between us let my sister go."

"Arquilio," the woman cried "Why is he doing this?"

"I'll tell you why, Maritza your brother my oldest friend in the entire world has violated my trust. He has stolen millions from me, Maritza, and I want my money back."

"Rquilio, is this true? Give him his money don't be stupid.

"It's not true, Maritza I haven't stolen anything-from him.

"We'll get to the bottom of this" Las Casas nodded to Micaela, who put her gun in her belt, grabbed Maritza's dress with both hands, and ripped it off her body.

"What?" Maritza s h r i e k e d "Stop! Leave me alone!"

Micaela pulled a knife from her boot and cut off Maritza's bra and panties. She thrust her leg into the back of Maritza's knees and forced her to the floor- Micaela then drew her pistol and pressed it against the blonde woman's temple.

"Jorge! Stop! What are you doing?" Maritza sobbed.

"One-way or another, your brother is going to return my money. You're going to help me convince him to cooperate."

"I didn't steal your money!" Crespo screamed. Dana was shaking in her chair, she wanted to see Crespo dead or in prison, but as far as she knew the sister was innocent. Maybe not entirely innocent, but not guilty of any crime other than living off the proceeds of her brother's criminal conduct. She sat rigid and upright with her hands tightly pressed together. Her knuckles were white from the tension. Her lip was quivering, and a tear was forming in the corner of her eye.

Micaela poked Maritza in the spine with the barrel of her pistol.

"Face on the floor," she ordered.

Sobbing, Maritza collapsed to the floor. Micaela stepped over her and stood with her boots on either side of Maritza's torso. She bent at the waist, grabbed two fistfuls of Maritza's hair, and pulled her up on to all fours.

"You're going to service my men until your brother tells me where I can find my god damned money," Las Casas snarled" If you refuse, Na will splatter his brains all over this room."

Na pressed her pistol against Crespo's ear for emphasis Las Casas motioned to the two men furthest from the table. They walked to the centre of the room and stood at opposite ends of Maritza's four point position. Na stood over Maritza and held her by the hair while the men unfastened their belts and dropped their trousers.

"Jorge, stop this insanity," Crespo pleaded "I don't have your money."

"Arquilio, the next word I want to hear out of your mouth is you telling me where I can find my money anything else, and Maritza dies."

Crespo's mouth snapped shut.

Na jerked back on Maritza's hair sobbing, she opened her mouth to accept the rigid penis poking her forehead. The man grabbed her by the sides of her head and eased his cock into her mouth. The other man placed his boot between Maritza's knees and nudged her legs apart. He slapped her ass and then knelt behind her. It took him several strokes to work his cock into her pussy, but in a matter of seconds, he was pounding his entire length in and out of her.

"You can make this stop, Rquilio you know what you have to do."

Crespo opened his mouth, but no words came out. He ground his teeth and stared at Las Casas.

The man fucking Maritza from behind finished first, he increased his speed, grunted several times, and then shot his load inside her. He backed away, pulled up his pants, and stood to the side while the other man jabbed his cock in and out of Maritza's mouth. Semen dripped from her gaping pussy and puddled on the floor between her knees. Within minutes the second man was grunting and spilling his seed in the woman's throat. He withdrew his cock and then held his hand over Maritza's face, forcing her to swallow his entire load.

The two men returned to their positions Las Casas motioned for the next two men to take their places just as before, one man shoved his cock between Maritza's lips while the second man entered her from behind. These two seemed to have participated in this type of activity before, or perhaps they worked out a strategy while watching their predecessors. This pair established a rhythm, alternately plunging their hard cocks in and out of Maritza such that one man entered just as the other withdrew. Maritza's pussy was slick with the cum from the first man, so there was less friction as the second shaft plunged in and out of her.

Crespo stood in stony silence, his dark eyes blazing in Las Casas directions light smile formed on the corner of Las Casas' mouth. He locked eyes with Na and then tipped his head to the right, Na pushed Crespo's temple with the barrel of her gun, forcing him to turn his head and watch as his younger sister was simultaneously impaled in her pussy and mouth-Crespo closed his eyes and groaned.

The man fucking Maritza's face came first taking a cue from his predecessor, he also held her mouth shut after withdrawing his cock, forcing her to swallow a second load of semen. The man fucking her pussy followed a few minutes later. He smacked her ass several times as he pumped his cum into her slit, where it mixed with the remnants from the first load. When they were through the two men stepped away and returned to their posts.

Maritza looked up at Las Casas, her face was red and puffy drool was running from the corners of her mouth, and black eyeliner streaked her cheeks. She tried to get off her hands and flex her arms, but

Micaela pushed her to the floor with the tip of her gun-Las Casas signaled, and two more men assumed their positions around Maritza.

The third pair wasted no time filling Maritza from both ends. This pair seemed to be in a race; their hips were a blur as they pumped her with lightning quickness. In less than five minutes they were both zipping their pants and stepping away.

The fourth pair took their places. The man in front shoved his cock to the back of Maritza's throat while his partner worked his cock into her pussy Maritza's eyes widened and her jaw went slack. She pushed the cock out of her mouth and looked up.

"This one, I can feel," she said. "Finally, Jorge, you bring me a real man."

Na pulled Maritza's hair and slapped her face just as the man standing behind her buried the full length of his shaft inside the naked woman's dripping cunt.

"Ungh! He's almost as big as you, Jorge."

Maritza s m i l e d and winked at Jorge, then swallowed the entire cock that was poking just below her eye. For the first time all day, she sucked with enthusiasm. Her lips created a seal around the shaft while her cheeks collapsed as a result of the suction she was applying to the swollen head. She bobbed back and forth on the stiff cock without the necessity of direction from the owner or the threat of violence from

Micaela. She sucked and slurped until the cock exploded in her mouth. When the man's balls were emptied, he stepped to the side. Maritza opened her mouth to show Las Casas the semen pooled on her tongue then closed her lips and swallowed the load. "Yum," she said "Now fuck me, big boy Give it to me."

The man fucking her from behind responded instantly predecessors' semen out of her hole with every thrust back into position with a jerk of her hair.

He pushed his thick shaft in and out, pushing his Maritza dipped her head, but Micaela snapped it. "Fuck me! Deeper! Fuck me harder!"

The man was thrusting his heavy shaft with increasing force, rocking Maritza's body with every impact of his groin against her soft, curvy ass.

"That's it! Fuck me hard!"

Maritza rocked her ass backward to meet the man's thrusts every impact created a loud smacking noise that echoed throughout the room.

"Give it to me! Harder! Fuck me like a real man!" The fat cock rammed in and out of her pussy sweat was dripping off the man's face. Large stains appeared on the back of his shirt and beneath the underarms. His fingers dug into the soft flesh of Maritza's hips as he pummeled her pussy with increasing ferocity.

After several minutes of sustained fury he let out a wail that no one in the room could ignore.

"Ahhhhhhhhhhhhhhhhh!" he screamed "Unghhhhhhhhhhhhhhhh!"

When he stood, a river of semen flowed from Maritza's cunt fresh puddle of the slippery fluid formed between her knees.

"Thank you, Jorge," Maritza teased "That one was good too bad you had to go through six men before you found one who knew how to fuck."

"Maritza," Las Casas growled.

"He fucked me like you used to remember when you used to sneak into my room and fuck me after my parents were asleep?"

"Jorge!" Crespo shouted "Chingòn!"

"Not now, Maritza" Las Casas glared at the naked woman drenched in semen and saliva.

"You used to come up to my room and eat my pussy until I was gushing all over the sheets. Then you would fuck me so hard with that big cock until I was nearly bleeding. I think you're the reason that I can't have children."

His dark eyes blazing with anger, Las Casas roared at Micaela "Take her away!"

Micaela pulled Maritza to her feet and dragged her to the door.

"Aren't you going to fuck me? You said I had the sweetest pussy you ever tasted. Why don't you want me anymore, Jorge? Do you think that cunt sitting with you can fuck you better than I did? She's nothing but a whore."

Dana's face flushed, she looked down to avoid Maritza's gaze.

"Micaela!" Las Casa barked. Micaela stopped with her hand on the door.

"Put her on the boat Lock her in one of the rear staterooms she's going back to Colombia with us." "What are you doing with her?" Crespo asked. "We're finally going to be together" Maritza laughed.

"She's going to a whorehouse in Medellṣn," Las Casas said "Say goodbye to your sister, Rquilio." "You cock sucking bastard! Let her go! She doesn't have anything to do with this! Please, Jorge!" "Take heraway."

"She never did anything to you! Jorge! Leave her alone! This is between us Let's settle this man to man."

"When you return my $30 million, we can talk about a settlement. Until then, there will be no bargaining."

Micaela dragged Maritza through the door and out of the house. Dana looked around the room and wondered in which direction her future would lie. I am going to end up like Maritza, fucked literally and figuratively? Staring down the barrel of a gun, like Crespo? Or can I work my way up to security, like Micaela and Na? I have training. He thinks I'm just a whore, but I'm really a cop almost. Is there any way for me out of this mess?

Ten minutes later the door opened and Micaela resumed her position behind Las Casas. "Arquilio, you surprise me," Las Casas said

"How so?"

"I would have thought that your sister was worth more to you than $30 million."

"I don't have your money, Jorge."

"That is your story, the records tell a different story" "Give me some time I can explain."

"Time is the one thing you do not have, old friend."

"Then kill me and get it over with Go ahead, shoot me you're going to anyway."

"I'm disappointed in you, Rquilio. If I kill you, I will never see my money again that is, as you know, the only thing keeping you alive."

"Then we are atan impasse."

"Not quite I still have another card to play."

Las Casas nodded to Micaela, who left the room once again. She returned a few moments later with a captive bound and wearing a black bag over her head.

Micaela forced the prisoner to the floor and removed the bag slender woman in a crisp white dress trimmed in delicate lace and eyelet, knelt on the floor with her hands tied behind her back. Her glossy black hair was styled in long curls that held up despite the humid climate. Her skin was the color of honey beautiful as could be expected of a Miss Colombia finalist a listlessness that permeated her being.

Her makeup was impeccable as her eyes, however were glazed and there was,

"Natalia!" Crespo shouted. "No! You monster! What have you done to her?"

"Arquilio, if anyone is going to share in the fruits of your treachery, it would no doubt be your lovely wife. Who else, then, should be responsible for deciding your fate?"

"How did you find her? What did you do to her?" "My friend, you know I have a network of eyes and ears all over this hemisphere. Did you really think there was anywhere on this planet that you could hide her from me?"

"Jorge, please leave her out of this."

"You know I can't do that I didn't have my men combing all of South America for her just so I could let her go."

"No, Jorge, no please."

"You've already established that your sister is not worth $30 millions a result, she will live out the rest of her days as a prostitute. How about your wife? Is she worth $30 million?"

"I don't have your $30 million please, you have to believe me."

"The problem, my friend, is that I don't believe you."

Micaela cut the dress from Natalia she barely moved as the clothing was stripped from her body.

"What's wrong with her?" Crespo asked.

"She was a little frantic hell, she's your wife, you know how she can be when things don't go exactly her way."

"What did you door her, Jorge?" "We've kept her subdued with heroin" "Motherfucker!"

"She'll be fine we' ve managed the dosage of course, she'll eventually have to go through withdrawal if she comes off it, that is." "Jorge, stop this."

"Pay me my money." "There is no money." "We'll see about that."

"What are you going to do, have the rest of your men fuck her?" "Not the rest of my men just one."

"Who?" "Franklin."

"No!" Crespo's eyes shot daggers at Las Casas

"That negrito is not touching my wife!" Las Casas picked up his phone.

"Mr Davis, I need you downstairs."

He tucked the phone in his shirt pocket. "You're running out of time, Rquilio" "Bastard! Mother fucker!"

"Why didn't you come to me, Rquilio? I could have had the accountant find new income streams for you. He's a genius when it comes to creating wealth all you had to do was talk to me."

"I told you already I don't have your god-damned money."

The door opened and Franklin Davis stepped into the room.

"Franklin," Las Casas said "The woman on the floor Enjoy."

"Thank you, boss there any restrictions?" "None."

Davis unbuttoned his shirt and threw it to the floor. He had shoulders like a linebacker and his chiselled chest was as big as a barrel. He kicked off his shoes and then pulled off his socks. He took off his pants and threw them on top of the shoes. His thighs were as thick as Natalia's waist. His arms bulged. His stomach was flat, solid, and deeply ridged. His neck looked like a knotted cord. Even his butt looked firmer than two bowling balls standing naked, he was six feet of solid, ebony muscle. His most impressive muscle was the one hanging between his legs.

Dana gasped, He's huge he makes even Alexander and Las Casas look small. "This is your last chance, Rquilio," Las Casas said.

"I don't have your money." "She's all yours, Franklin." "Thank you, boss," Davis said.

"You've earned it, my friend, I am in your debt." Davis strutted to the wall and picked up a heavy upholstered chair. He sauntered to the centre of the room and set the chair on the floor next to Natalia. He helped her to her feet, and then set her on the chair.

"Give me your knife," he said to Micaela,

"Don't you touch her! I'll kill you!" Crespo screamed. "You black bastard mother fucker!"

Davis ignored Crespo's threats. He extended his hand to Micaela, who hesitated for a second before drawing the knife from her boot and handing it to Davis afraid of what might happen next. Dana lowered her gaze, covered her eyes with her hand, and turned her head to the side. She would have leapt at the opportunity to flee the room if one were provided.

Davis leaned over Natalia, grabbed her wrists, and cut the rope binding them together. He straightened his back and handed the knife to Micaela, who replaced it in her boot. Davis brushed the stray hairs from Natalia's face, then rested a hand on her cheek. He tilted her head upward and looked into her eyes. She stared back at him with a vacant, unblinking expression. Her lips parted, but no sound came from her mouth. Davis leaned forward and placed a gentle kiss on her forehead.

"Please forgive me," he whispered in her ear, "I mean you no harm."

Davis knelt on the floor facing Natalia. He pulled her ass to the edge of the chair and then flipped her legs over his shoulders. He lowered his face to her hairless pussy and licked her slit from top to bottom. Davis worked his tongue between her folds, teasing every surface and drinking every drop of juice that his efforts produced. He licked up and down both sides of her fleshy petals, flattened his tongue and probed her canal, and then flicked the tip of his tongue over her tiny pink clit.

Natalia tilted her chin upward. Her eyes rolled to the back of her head and the palms of her hands pushed down on Franklin's shaved scalp. She arched her back while her thighs closed and squeezed Franklin's skull Natalia's mouth opened, releasing a scream that rattled off every surface in the cavernous room.

"aaaaaaaahhhhhhhhhhhhhhh!"   she   cried "h!aaaaaaaaahhhhhhhhh!"

Davis continued licking Natalia's screams rose another octave, and then dissolved into silence. The hands slapping the back of Franklin's skull became fists pounding his shoulders while Natalia's feet waved back and forth as though she were running in space.

Davis finally relented, he stood up, grabbed Natalia by the waist, and lifted her off the chair. He sat down and then lowered her onto his lap. With her eyes closed and her back to Davis, Natalia reached between her legs and grasped his fully erect cock. She rubbed the head against her clit, and then adjusted herself so that the purple mushroom was positioned against her pink opening. She slowly lowered her torso to Franklin's lap as her pussy stretched to accommodate the enormous black invader. Natalia bounced up and down on Franklin's lap, taking another inch of thick black cock with every descent of her ass.

"Ungh!" she groaned "Ungh!"

Davis placed his huge hands on Natalia's tiny waist and lifted her with his powerful arms. The slender woman moaned every time she slid down his shaft. Natalia's breathing became more ragged as Davis increased the pace holding her with both hands, he slid her up and down his shaft as though he were masturbating.

Davis paused for a second to reach under Natalia's thighs. He pushed her legs up to her chest, smashing her knees against her small, firm breasts. He thrust in and out of her until her grunts became a long, sustained moan. He untucked her legs and then spun her around so that she was facing him man handling the small woman like a giant with a toy doll. Davis pointed her feet to the sky so that she was folded in half on his lap.

Holding Natalia's folded form in his strong arms, and with his cock impaling her tight, slick, pussy. Davis stood up while continuing to thrust his organ in and out of her small body. With his cock still inside her. Davis walked to the edge of the room and pressed Natalia's back against the wall. Her feet resting on his shoulders, Davis thrust in and out of her, pushing his manhood deeper with every motion.

Dana squirmed in her chair Oh my god! I've never seen anything like that. This is so fucking hot! Her face flushed red as she fought the urge to slip a finger into her pussy.

The muscles on Franklin's back glistened with sweat, his buttocks clenched and unclenched as he rolled his hips forward and backward.

"Unghhhhhh!" Natalia cried out "Fill me!"

Natalia leaned forward and pressed her lips against Franklin's chin. She bounced her head all over his face, searching for his mouth. When she found it, she pressed her lips against his and forced her tongue between his teeth. Suspended between the hard wall and Franklin's harder chest, Natalia wrapped her arms around his head kissed him with same urgency as his cock slamming in and out of her pussy.

Crespo refused to watch. Instead, he glared at Las Casas with a dark fury that was only restrained by Na's pistol jammed into his ear.

Las Casas glanced from Crespo to Natalia and Davis, and then back to Crespo on amused smile creased his lips as he watched Crespo suffer. Davis was giving Natalia the fucking of her life, and Crespo was unable to stop it.

"hhhhhhhhhh!" Natalia's cry filled the room" Ungh! aaaaaaahhhhhhh!"

Davis thrust in and out of Natalia with a renewed fury every thrust was punctuated with a loud grunt.

"Unh! Unh! Unh! Unh!"

Davis and Natalia's raucous duet reached a crescendo as Natalia bit the big man's lip, he thrust into her a final time, and then backed away from the wall. Natalia collapsed to the floor as a flood of semen poured from her gaping hole.

Davis bent over and kissed her cheek, then scooped her up in his arms and cradled her. Natalia was panting; tears ran down her cheeks as she struggled to catch her breath.

"Franklin," Las Casas said

"Yes."

"Take her to your room." "And then?"

"She's yours."

"Thank you, boss."

Leaving their clothes behind, Davis carried Natalia's limp, naked body out of the room.

"Fucker!" Crespo screamed, "I'll kill you!" He glared first at the retreating Davis, and then at Las Casas, Micaela, and Na in turn "and you! and you! and you! You're dead! You're all dead! All of you! Dead! Do you hear me? Dead! I'll kill all of you god damned mother fucking bastards!"

"This is your fault, Rquilio tell me what I want to know and the torture ends" "I don't have the money I'm telling you, I didn't steal $30 million from you." "You keep saying that, yet I am not convinced."

"Chingžn, mother fucker, I don't know what you are talking about!"

Las Casas pulled the phone from his pocket and tapped the screen.

Oh God, what now? that bastard is going to destroy his entire family just to hold on to the money. "Curious choice of words, Rquilio here you are

147

prostrated before me, while every man in this room has a gun pointed at your head, and you're making threats? You should be begging me for your life." "You're insane, Jorge I don't care what they're telling you, I don't have your money."

"Rquilio, I know you have always thought yourself to be smarter than me and I admit, in some ways you are, but your attempt to part words with me is insulting."

"What are you talking about?"

"I notice that you are very careful to state that you don't have my money, I believe you. We've searched the entire house, and it's clear that the money is not here. In this case, however, what you are not saying is just as revealing as what you do say."

"You're talking in circles, old friend."

"And you are engaged in a game of deception. It is a game that you will lose. What you are not saying is that you have not stolen from me."

"Jorge, it's obvious that is what I meant."

"What is obvious is that you are a thief, a liar, and a traitor."

"You mis judge me." "Do I?"

The door opened and two men walked in leading another woman with a black bag over her head. This woman was wearing clothing like the first two, but was much heavier than her predecessors. Her knee- length embroidered dress covered a plump but shapely form featuring full breasts, a round belly, an ample backside, and thick legs that tapered to delicate feet. She held tightly to her captors' arms as she tottered across the room. Her heavy breasts swayed from side to side with every tentative step, while her ample butt jiggled suggestively.

Las Casas rose from his chair and walked to the center of the room. He stopped next to the captive woman and placed his hand on the top of the bag.

"Minute ago, old friend, you called me 'mother fucker,' "Las Casas sneered at Crespo. "Do you remember?"

"Of course, and I'll say it again Mother fucker."

"Your words were prophetic."

Las Casas pulled the bag off the woman's head, revealing an older woman in her late 50s with short auburn hair, brown eyes, and a stern expression.

"Mamá!" Crespo screamed,

Oh god! Oh god oh, god. That fucking asshole can't let his mother be raped, can he? Talk Please talk, it's time for this to end. Just talk and Las Casas will let her go, I know he will. Don't make him do it. Please please, just tell him where the money is "Goddamn you, Jorge!" Crespo shouted "Let her go!"

"That's up to you," Las Casas said "Tell me where my money is, and I won't touch her." "I'll kill you! You're dead! You're a dead man, Jorge! You're dead!"

"You're an idiot."

Las Casas reached for the zipper on the back of the woman's dress. He pulled it all the way down, then helped the dress fall to the floor.

"I'm very sorry, Josefina, that your son has put you in this situation."

"Jorge, my son is many things. He is a criminal and a murderer-I know that. His glamorous lifestyle -just like yours is built upon his participation in an international criminal enterprise. I am not blind to my son's sins, Jorge. Barring some kind of miraculous intervention, when his days are over his soul will rot in hell for all eternity-as will yours. But my son loves me, and he would not allow me to suffer if he could prevent it. Whatever it is that you believe he has taken from you, I'm sure that you are mistaken."

"I wish that were true, Señora I wish that were true. But everyone has a price, and Rquilio has determined his that he would allow his mother to stand naked in front of all these men must tell you that you do not know him like you think you do."

"I know my son, Jorge I know what he would do for me, I can do no less for him. Do to me what you will, but I'm telling you that my son has not done whatever offence you believe he committed."

"So be it."

Las Casas unfastened her bra and threw it on the floor with her dress. Her back, shoulders, and even her heavy breasts were marked with indentations from the bra. Her dark areolas framed small nipples that pointed to the floor. He pulled her panties down her hips, revealing an ample ass and a full black bush.

He took a step back and removed his shirt and shoes. He untied his pants and let them fall to the floor.

"No! Mamá! Don't do it! You bastard! You're dead, Jorge! Do you hear me? Dead!"

"Silence, Rquilio! If he says one more word, Na, put a bullet in his skull."

"It's OK, son, I've been violated by worse men than this, I'll survive."

Crespo put his head down and sobbed.

I can't watch this Dana looked down at the table. She squeezed her eyes shut, and then clenched her teeth and put her hand over her brow as a shield. What a bastard, what a cop killing, sister, wife and mother hating bastard. I hope Las Casas kills him.

Las Casas stepped in front of Josefina and put his hands on her shoulders. He guided her to her knees and then offered her his flaccid cock. She closed her eyes, took it in her mouth, and sucked. In a matter of seconds, it started to swell. In less than a minute it reached its full length and girth Josefi. Na's cheeks bulged as the thick shaft stretched her lips and filled her mouth.

Jorge withdrew his erect cock from Josefina's mouth. He helped her to her feet and then led her to the chair where Davis had fucked Natalia a few minutes earlier. Las Casas nudged her into position on the chair. He directed her to kneel on the seat with her back toward him, and to lean forward with her arms wrapped around the chair back.

"You can't look at my face, Jorge?" she asked.

"I prefer to remember you as someone other than the whore mother of a traitor and thief," Las Casas responded.

"Whatever will help you sleep at night."

Josefina clung to the back of the chair. Her face was pressed against the fabric while her drooping breasts and soft belly sagged almost to the seat cushion. Las Casas stood behind her and lined up the head of his cock with the entrance to Josefina's pussy. He rubbed the head up and down her slit several times, and then took a step backward. He spit on his fingers and then parted Josefina's pink folds with his moist digit.

"What's wrong, Jorge, I'm not wet enough for you? I guess you don't turn me on that much. I prefer men with some intelligence."

Las Casas thrust his fingers in and out of her pussy. When he was satisfied with the moisture in her canal, he removed his fingers and replaced them with his cock.

"Damn, I was starting to like that. It's probably all downhill from here."

"Woman, you talk too much."

Las Casas pushed forward, burying his entire cock inside her in one hard thrust.

"Ungh!" she grunted.

Las Casas pulled out so that just the head was still inside her, then pushed in again with even more force.

"Let's see if you can talk while I'm pounding your fat old pussy" "Are you going to pound me with your finger?"

Smack!

Las Casas slapped Josefina's ass cheek with the palm of his hand. He grabbed her fleshy hips and slammed his cock in and out of her pussy. Her heavy tits swayed and her hanging belly jiggled with every thrust. Las Casas pulled all the way out and then slammed his groin against her fat ass over and over.

The sound of his body smashing into her backside filled the room.

"I thought you were going to use your cock," Josefina taunted. "I've been fucked harder by drunken old men in a nursing home."

Smack! Smack!

Las Casas slapped both ass cheeks.

"Are you trying to turn me on now? That little appendage of yours sure isn't doing the job."

Smack! Smack! Smack! Smack!

Las Casas slapped both cheeks until they were red

"Is that all you've got? I can almost feel your hands slapping my ass at least I'm getting something from you."

What is she doing? Is she trying to get herself killed?

Dana raised her eyes and parted her fingers. She saw Las Casas reach for the woman's hair and pull her head backward. He was thrusting in and out of Josefina's pussy faster and harder than he ever had with her. The older woman's raised backside was as wide as the chair, and apparently more cushioned. She absorbed the thrusts of his thick cock with ease Josefina continued to taunt Las Casas.

"Can someone turn on the TV? I'm falling asleep." Las Casas pulled her hair again, forcing her to look straight up at the ceiling. He spat on her face, then pushed her face into the cushion, Josefina turned her face to the side.

"If you're planning to fuck me sometime today, why don't you eat my pussy first? If you're just going to tickle my clit, then don't bother. I'll wait for a real man to show up."

Please stop taunting him. Please this isn't helping.

"Josefina," Las Casas said, "shut your fucking-mouth."

Las Casas pulled his cock out of her pussy, placed the tip against her asshole, and pushed. He grabbed her wrists and pulled back on her arms for leverage The helmet pressed against her unprepared sphincter-it resisted for several seconds before surrendering to the brute force burrowing its way inside her.

"Ungh! Woooooo!" Josefina groaned" So that's how you're going to play it."

"Maricžn!" Crespo shouted." You fuck like a faggot!"

"Are you afraid that I might cause her to abort one of your siblings?" "Let me loose so I can kill you!"

"Shut up, traitor Watch me fuck your mother's fat ass."

Las Casas pulled on Josefina's wrists, causing sharp pains to ripple through her arms and back.

"I thought you were a man, Jorge you fuck like a monkey."

Enraged by her words, Las Casas pulled on her arms and slammed his cock in and out of her asshole her body shook with every thrust.

"Is that all you've got?"

What is she doing? That old woman is crazy

"Harder! Fuck me harder! Fuck me like a real man!"

Las Casas pounded the old woman's ass with all the force he could generate. Sweat dripped off his forehead as he thrust in and out of the woman eyes in the room were focused on Las Casas as he drilled the woman's fat ass with a level of anger and violence none had ever witnessed.

Dana tried her best to comprehend the situation.

She hated Crespo for everything he had done, and everything that he was allowing to happen. What a greedy bastard! Allowing his sister, wife and mother to be taken so brutally. What kind of code do these people live by? How would detective Trujillo's widow feel? Would this make up for the loss of her beautiful husband? Such a handsome man. Is this justice?

"Fuck me, you pussy! Fuck my fat ass! Fuck it hard!" Josefina screamed.

"Ungh!" Las Casas grunted as the cum rose up from his balls "Ungh! Mmmmmmm! Ungh!" "Now!" Josefina shouted.

Dana looked up just as Las Casas emptied his balls into Josefina's bowels out of the corner of her eye she saw Crespo lurch free of Na, spin around, and knock the gun from her hand. Both of them dove on the floor to retrieve it. Crespo fell on the pistol, and then a shot rangout all eyes in the room turned to see Dana holding Las Casas' gun. The barrel was pointed at Crespo, who was laying on the floor in a pool of blood.

"No!" Josefina screamed "Mi hijo!"

Dana got up from behind the table and hurried over to Crespo. She kicked the gun away from him and then lowered her ear to his mouth. His breathing was faint, but he was still alive. She placed her lips against his ear and whispered so that only he could hear.

"Die, cop killer."

Crespo's eyes widened and a croak escaped from his throat Dana placed the barrel to his temple and fired Crespo's head exploded.

"No! No! No!" Josefina shrieked "Rquilio! My son!"

"Take her out of here," Las Casas said to Micaela

Micaela signaled for another man to join her and the two of them dragged Josefina from the room.

Las Casa put on his pants and walked over to Dana, Dana handed him the pistol and then broke into tears.

"Well, well, well," Las Casas said" It seems that I was right about you. There is more to you than meets the eye."

"I'm sorryI didn't he was going for the gun I" "It's OK, lovely lady, it's OK you saved my life." "But I killed him."

"He was already dead."

"But your money now."

"He wasn't going to tell me where it was once he let his sister get used and didn't talk, I knew he was never going to give anything away."

"But how."

"Davis and the accountant will find it, I have faith in them."

The door opened and a fully-clothed Davis entered with another man.

"Lydia, you know Franklin already I'd like you to meet my accountant, Mateo Hernandez Mateo, this is Lydia Zapata, Ms Zapata will be working for us in a very important capacity."

Hernandez extended his hand.

"Pleased to meet you, Lydia" "Likewise."

Dana took his hand and looked up at his face-He had a warm smile that no doubt melted women's hearts and opened their thighs, short black hair, a black mustache and goatee, and dazzling blue eyes.

That face I've seen those eyes before, that's Detective Trujillo!

"Sit down, Detective," Captain Hendricks said "Do either of you have any idea why I asked you to meet with me?"

"No" Detective Harris fidgeted with the files in his hand and refused to look Hendricks in the eye.

"Is this about our closed file reports?" Detective

Espinoza asked" I think I can explain that dips you know, we've both been in court testifying on the O'Mara prosecution. The assistant State's Attorney has been monopolizing our time this month with briefings and strategy sessions. Everyday she's had at least one of us tied up until after midnight for two straight weeks. We haven't been out on the street as much as we'd like to be."

"That's not what I'm talking about" Hendricks took off his glasses and glared at Espinoza. "Cadet Lvarado hasn't reported to the cademy in over a week. Do either of you know anything about her absence?"

"No, Sir," Harris answered.

"When did it become my responsibility to baby sit cadets?" Zac sneered, "I have cases to close."

"It just seems rather suspicious to me that the very person you two recommended for this covert operation turned up missing a week before it was scheduled to take place."

"Then I suppose you made the correct decision when you elected not to approve it," Espinoza said. "Cadet Lvarado did not impress me as the type

that would drop out of the program just weeks before graduation," Hendricks countered, "I got the impression that she's made of sterner stuff than that." "Maybe she had personal issues, you know?" Espinoza looked out the window" stuff at home boyfriend problems who knows?"

Harris' head snapped up, he shot a quick look at Espinoza and then bent his neck again.

"Is there something you want to add, Harris?" "No, Sir."

"Her instructors are baffled, she's near the top of her class, they tell me. Her phone goes straight to voice mail. It makes no sense. Unless she went out of town, for some unknown reason."

"We haven't spoken to her, Captain," Espinoza said.

"Run by her apartment, talk to her family find out whatever you can and report back to me" "Yes, Sir" Harris looked up at Hendricks. His eyes were moist.

"Are we excused?" Espinoza asked. "Get out of here."

Dana sat in the stateroom on Las Casas' boat, picking at the plate of food in front of her Las Casas was in the house meeting with his advisors, leaving her alone for the third consecutive evening.

After killing Crespo, Dana ran out of the house and holed herself up on the yacht. The twins took turns watching over her, but Dana refused to talk to them or anyone else. She cried herself to sleep that night, not even waking up when Las Casas joined her in the bed just before dawn. She awoke the next morning with his arms around her and his erection poking her in the back, but she did not respond, and he did not press the issue.

Dana spent the next day alone on the yacht. The twins continued to check on her, but otherwise she was left alone. Plates of food were brought to her at meal time, but she ate very little.

In the evening, she asked Na to bring her a bottle of champagne. Na returned with a bottle of Dom Perignon, which Dana finished in less than an hour. She asked Micaela to bring her a second bottle, which she took with her to the hot tub. Na found her an hour later, her chin resting on her chest and the empty bottle floating in the frothy water. Na helped Dana out of the tub and dragged her limp body to the stateroom. The brunette removed Dana's bikini and put her to bed. Dana was snoring before Na could turn off the lights.

Dana awoke the next day with Micaela sleeping at her side Las Casas spent the night in the house and left Micaela to watch over her. Dana spent most of that day in bed with the curtains drawn and the lights off. Her epic hangover was compounded by the gentle rocking of the boat one point she considered relocating to the house, but the searing pain she experienced when she tried to stand ended that thought.

It was late in the afternoon when she was finally able to sit up. She didn't stir when breakfast or lunch was brought to her, but by dinner time she was feeling hungry. The twins brought her a plate of churrasco, rice, and tostones. There was also bowl of diced fruit and a basket of bread. Dana picked at the churrasco, nibbled on the tostones, and ignored the rice and bread. She ate most of the fruit, leaving little for the twins.

"El Jefe says that if you don't come out of here by tomorrow morning, then we're supposed to drag you out," Micaela said Dana looked up from her food and saw Micaela glaring at her.

"Stop lying," Na scolded.

"I'm not feeling well," Dana said.

"We know," Micaela said "We heard you this morning puking in the head. How much did you drink last night?"

"I don't know," Dana answered" Two bottles of champagne? Three? I'm not sure."

"First time you ever killed someone?" Na extended her hand to rub Dana's arm. "Yes."

"It gets easier," Micaela said.

"Have the two of you killed before?"

"Yes," Na answered. She dropped her head and looked at the table, then peered out the window.

"Several times. The first time was the hardest pulling the trigger was easy, but I froze when the body hit the ground. I would have been captured if my sister wasn't there to pull me out of it"

"Who was it?"

"Maggot," Micaela sneered.

"Party politician who was scheming with El General's rivals to discredit him," corrected Na.

"The world is a better place without him" Micaela said "El General would have been ruined if my sister hadn't eliminated him when she did."

"My sister is over stating things."

"And if it's any consolation, Lydia, Crespo deserved to die" Micaela looked deep into Dana's eyes "El Jefe was going to kill him whether he talked or not. You did him a service and proved your loyalty at the same time."

"Then why is he still angry?"

"He's angry at the betrayal," Micaela said "He and Crespo had a lot of history together. Las Casas was a small time dealer in Barranquilla when he recruited Crespo a 13-year old street kid as a mule twenty years later, Las Casas is the biggest supplier in the Western Hemisphere and Crespo is his righthand man Crespo's treachery was devastating."

"He's grateful for your intervention," Na added

"It doesn't seem that way."

"Then consider this," Micaela said "Tomorrow you start training with us."

"Training?"

"You're being promoted from whore to security." Micaela smiled at Dana "You'll get to guard his body in more ways than one."

Wonderful now I'll never get a chance to go home. Las Casas slipped into the stateroom and crept into bed without turning on the lights. He did his best to avoid waking Dana, but the effort was pointless. She was already awake.

"What time is it?" she asked.

"Two-thirty." "You didn't."

Did I wake you? I was trying not to disturb you" I couldn't sleep."

"You're still upset. Would you like a sleeping pill?"

"No, I have to work through this" "Lydia."

"Yes"

"You did the right thing. If Crespo had gotten his hands on that gun, who knows what could have happened?"

"His hands were tied, Jorge."

"That made him even more dangerous. He's killed before under even more dire circumstances. He had the instincts of an animal and you know, an animal is always most dangerous when cornered."

"Still, my first shot stopped him, I didn't have to kill him."

"If you hadn't, someone else would have had to.

You finished what you started, I'm proud of you."

Las Casas wrapped an arm around Dana and pulled her body against his, she felt tears welling up in her eyes, and her throat seemed to develop a lump bigger than her fist. She turned her face into the pillow so that he wouldn't know she was crying.

"It's OK, Lydia, it's OK" Las Casas ran his fingers through Dana's hair." You put down a rabid animal, you probably saved my life. I've never been more impressed by any woman than I was at that moment I wanted to kiss you."

Dana turned her face toward Las Casas.

"Do you really mean that?" She struggled to force the words from her constricted throat.

"Absolutely."

Dana bent her neck downward. Her heart was racing, and she wasn't sure why conflicting emotions were swirling around inside her head. Las Casas's words and his gentle tone calmed her fears and eased her loneliness, but at the same time produced a new sensation that she couldn't identify. She sifted through her feelings until it struck her. Without realising it, she had been longing for his approval. It wasn't enough that he had assigned the twins to watch over her and care for her basic needs. She needed more than his acknowledgment. She craved his attention. Deep inside, she was ecstatic that he had finally returned to her.

Dana raised her head and searched for Las Casas's face. She couldn't see well in the dark, but she could sense that his eyes were open and he was looking directly at her. She moved her face toward him. She brushed her lips against his mouth. Las Casas cradled her face in his hands and parted his lips just enough to taste her breath in his mouth. Dana slipped her tongue past his teeth. Las Casas inhaled sharply, then met her tongue with his own tentative probe. When she did not retreat, he shifted his weight and rolled his shoulder into Dana.

Dana realized he was trying to maneuver her onto her back, but instead of submitting, she placed her free hand on his shoulder and pushed.

"My turn," she whispered.

Las Casas resisted for a moment, but then gave in and rolled onto his back. Dana wasted no time climbing on top of him. She raised her ass off his groin, reached between her legs, and closed her fingers around his stiff shaft. Dana carefully lowered her crotch onto the tip of his bulbous cockhead. She immediately realized that she was not yet wet enough to accommodate the magnificent prick throbbing in her hand.

Dana paused and rubbed the head against her slit several times. Within seconds moisture was seeping from her channel and lubricating the thick head poised at the entrance to her vulva. She rubbed the head in the crease between her lips, and then slid the glistening head against her clit. She felt her skin getting warmer as little jolts of electricity made their presence known in the back of her brain.

"Mmmmmmm," Las Casas moaned.

The man's guttural tone snapped Dana out of her revery. She placed the swollen tip against her tight opening and lowered her weight onto Las Casas's cock. The head stretched her walls as it slid into her tunnel. She felt a familiar fullness that her body welcomed like a hot meal on a cold day. Dana placed her hands-on Las Casas chest and pushed up and down several times. With each descent, another inch of his thick shaft disappeared inside her body.

Once she had taken his entire cock, Dana lowered her chest to his. Her nipples pressed into his skin as her mouth once again searched for his lips. Dana brushed his long black hair from his forehead, and then kissed his chin, cheeks and nose. She pressed her lips hard against his mouth. Las Casas pulled her auburn hair away from her face and returned her kiss. She felt her heart racing as her body craved more of him.

Dana was revelling in the contact of her lips against Las Casas's mouth when she felt a ripple run through her torso. She squeezed her thighs together and felt Las Casas's cock throbbing in her tunnel. Quite by accident, she discovered that her clit was pressed against his pubic bone, and the slightest movement caused a shockwave to run from her pussy to the center of her brain. Every time she flexed her thighs another jolt raced through her. Las Casas's groans told her that he was enjoying the experience almost as much as she was. Dana continued squeezing, but she was having a difficult time maintaining her concentration. The feelings she was experiencing were unlike anything she had ever felt before.

The temptation to slide her pussy up and down on Las Casas's voluminous cock was becoming unbearable. She wanted to prolong the experience and see how high she could fly, but the urge to rush to orgasm was irresistible.

Thirty more seconds was all that Dana could take her need for relief overcame her interest in seeing how long she could hover on the event horizon of an ever-ascending climax. She buried her face in Las Casas's neck and rode his cock like a jockey riding a race horse down the back stretch of the Kentucky Derby.

Her tight body sliding up and down the thick shaft, each moan that escaped her throat was louder and longer than the one preceding it. Her orgasm was approaching like a brick wall and she was racing toward it with her foot on the accelerator. Her body was on fire like a circuit carrying ten times the electrical current it was designed to handle. Her ass rose up and down, slamming onto Las Casas' groin. The meaty cock filled and then vacated her pussy over and over. Her skin tingled as her mind soared higher and higher.

"Oohhhhhhhhhhhhhhhhhhhhhhh! Ungh!"

Dana screamed when her body slammed into the wall. Stars exploded in her brain and she was unable to breathe. She wanted to peel off her skin but she could not stop pumping her hips. Every movement sent more ripples of pleasure cascading through her body. She saw every colour all at once, and then everything went black.

She collapsed on Las Casas's chest. Her breathing resumed, but her heart continued racing. She tried to push up, but she did not have the strength to lift herself. She cradled his head and kissed his forehead. "Thank you," she panted." That was I can't describe it."

Dana hovered over Las Casas' face, leaving soft kisses on his cheeks, nose, and chin. When she reached his mouth she brushed her lips against his, then moved away when his lips parted. Las Casas responded by wrapping his arms around her back and then rolling his hips forward, pushing his cock another inch inside her.

"You you're still hard." Dana's eyes bulged and her jaw hung open "Sir."

"But--didn't you cum?"

"It would be impolite for a man to cum before his lady."

"I'm your lady now? I thought I was your whore" "Whore would never be allowed to look at me while we made love." "Last week--"

"Last week you were my whore, tonight you are my lady tomorrow--who knows?"

Dana leaned over and kissed Las Casas. She then rolled to the side, sliding off his cock and turning her back toward him. She tucked her knees against her chest and then reached behind for his arm.

"Hold me," she said.

Las Casas slid his arm over hers and pulled her toward him. His cock rested against the crack of her ass, but he made no move to enter her.

"Well?" she asked.

"Excuse me?"

"You're not finished yet."

Las Casas rolled his hips and adjusted his crotch so that the tip of his dick was pressed against moist Dana's lower lips.

"Not there," she said.

"I didn't think you liked it in your ass" "You know that's what you want" Dana rubbed her butt against his cock. "We don't have to do this."

Dana reached back grabbed his cock, and placed the head against her anus. She pushed her butt back against his cock. Her sphincter opened a fraction, allowing the tip to enter.

"Fuck my ass, Jorge you know you want to" "Lydia."

"I'm offering myself to you, all of me."

Las Casas grabbed her hips and pushed forward.

Dana's asshole opened just enough to take the head. "More," she said.

Las Casas drew back and then pushed forward again another inch of cock penetrated her ass.

"Come on Papi, fuck my ass, we both know that's what you want."

Once again Las Casas drew his hips back and then pushed forward. His cock was halfway up in her tight ass. He repeated the process until his groin was pressed against her butt cheeks.

"Tomorrow I'll still be your lady," Dana growled, "and also your whore."

"Mmmmm I like the soundof that."

Las Casas drew back and then thrust forward with more force.

"Ungh!" Dana grunted "Easy I'm still getting used to this" "You asked for it."

"I want to fuck you the way you like it destroy it" Las Casas settled into a slower rhythm.

But just because I'm giving you my ass doesn't mean I want you to.

He pulled his cock almost to the point of complete withdrawal, then pushed it back in an inch at a time. When his cock was completely buried in Dana's bowels he paused for a second, then repeated the motion.

"That's better," Dana purred.

"How does it feel?"

"It hurts--a little, not nearly as bad as a week ago" "Do you want me to stop?"

"Of course not." "But you just said"

"If I'm going to be your whore as well as your lady, I'm going to have to learn to get used to it."

"It's not necessary."

"Jorge, if you're not fucking my ass, you'll be burying that big cock in the twins, Or Maritza Or Josefina or some other whore."

"You're jealous?"

"No!" Dana slapped his thigh "Maybe a little You're surprised?" "I'm confused" "Good stay that way."

"Lydia--"

"Jorge, stop talking Pinch my nipples."

Las Casas wrapped his arms around Dana's torso.

His hands sought out her nipples, his strong fingers closed around each of her nubs, pulling and stretching them away from her chest. "Harder pinch them like this."

Dana put her hands over Las Casas fingers and squeezed with all her strength flash of pain shot from her nipples to her brain.

"Ungh!" she grunted "Bite my neck."

Las Casas pushed her hair away with his nose and then lowered his mouth to the back of her neck. He kissed and sucked, tasting the salty sweat coating her skin. He opened his mouth wider, and then pressed his teeth into the tender flesh just above the shoulder.

"Again!"

Las Casas closed his mouth, he felt her body squirm and gyrate as he bit her neck, pinched her nipples, and drove his cock into her ass--all at the same time.

"More!"

Las Casas didn't know if she wanted more pressure on her nipples, her neck, or in her ass. He pinched and pulled on her nipples until he feared he was tearing them off. He closed his mouth on her neck, but relented when he tasted her blood on his tongue.

"Fuck me."

Las Casas drew back and then thrust forward with the force of a bull.

"Ungh! Gentle be gentle."

The contradictory instructions were maddening. The deliberate pace he was trying to establish in her ass was becoming impossible to maintain as he complied with her demand for more pressure on her nipples and neck. His brain was screaming at his body, urging him to abandon all restraint and pound her ass like a wild animal roller coaster further away.

His balls were ready to explode as he soared on the rails of an emotional and sensual track. Every second seemed to bring him closer to his goal, yet the goal seemed to be moving.

"Ungh! That's it pinch them--harder!"

Las Casas felt like his balls would explode--or his head--never before had he rode to such a height of pleasure without climaxing. Pleasure became agony and agony became ecstasy. The slower he fucked the higher he soared and the more frustrated he became. Every stroke ratcheted the sensation another notch yet brought him no closer to release. The only outlets for his frustration were pinching her nipples and bitingher neck.

"Ungh! Now! Cum for me! Now!"

When her words hit his ears, Las Casas' last shred of self-control dissolved. He pulled his cock out and then thrust it into Dana's ass with all the force he could generate. His crotch slammed into her backside a dozen times before his mind exploded.

The cum shot up from his balls and through his shaft, filling her ass with spurt after spurt of thick cream. He slowed his pace and delivered another dozen thrusts, each with less velocity than the one it preceded. Thirty seconds later he stopped moving. His flaccid cock slid out of her ass followed a moment later by a stream of semen.

Dana lay in the bed, basking in the after glow of her own orgasm. Her ass was sore and would probably continue in that condition throughout the next morning and afternoon. She felt Las Casas's ragged breathing on her neck, and his heart pounding against her back. She pulled his arm around her and--for the first time in nearly two weeks--she felt safe.

Dana awoke to find herself alone in the bed. She wandered into the head and sat on the toilet while Las Casas showered. When she was done with her business she opened the shower door and joined Las Casas under the spray of hot water.

"Good morning, my lady." "Good morning, Papi."

"How are you feeling this morning?"

"My ass is sore, but other than that I feel amazing."

"Very good are you ready to start training today?" "If that's what you want, then sure, you going to supervise?"

"I'm afraid I have to go away for a fewdays." "Where are you going?"

"Tegucigalpa"

"The Capital? Why?"

"I have some business there that needs my attention."

"Why not send the accountant? Isn't that his responsibility now?"

"Yes, and no these are matters that were formerly handled by Crespo, and going forward they will be handled by Hernandez. But many of these men had long-standing relationships with Crespo, and I need to reassure them that their interests did not die with him."

"How long will you be gone?"

"Just a fewdays, three at the most."

"You're not going to visit any whores while you're away, are you?" "I'm not planning to. But you never know what may come up" "Looks to me like something is already coming up."

Dana reached between Las Casas' legs and grabbed his growing cock.

"What are you going to do about that?"

"That depends on how much time you have?"

"Not much."

"Then I guess I'm going to have to empty this quickly."

Las Casas pushed Dana to her knees and then guided her face to his crotch. She grabbed his cock with one hand, cupped his balls with the other, and swallowed the head. Five minutes later she was swallowing his load as he held her head and pumped his semen into her mouth.

Dana watched from the window as Las Casas boarded the helicopter. He carried a metal briefcase identical to the one he gave the General in Havanana handed him a small overnight bag and then closed the hatch, sealing him inside. The chopper lifted straight up into the air, turned toward the mainland, and disappeared behind the tropical canopy.

The rest of the day was spent training with the twins. Even though she had spent months learning self-defence and suppression methods at the cademy, the twins' proficiency with firearms and their mastery of combat techniques dwarfed Dana's rudimentary skills. By the end of the day she was battered and bruised, but she had a clear understanding of the gulf that existed between her abilities and those of the twins. She was looking forward to a hot bath, a quick meal, and an early bedtime so that she would be fully rested when her training resumed in the morning.

She had just settled into a steaming bath when there was a knock on the door second later the door opened and Micaela stuck her head into room.

"Get dressed," Micaela said.

"I just got in here" Dana protested, "I'm done for the day You don't get to torture me again until morning."

"You have a dinner appointment."

"Dinner? With who? Is Jorge back already?" "You'd love that, wouldn't you? No, Señor Las

Casas is still in Tegucigalpa." "Then who, may I ask?"

"Señor Hernandez is requesting that you join him He's expecting you in thirty minutes."

"Fuck! Can't you tell him. I'm not up to it? I really wanted to go to bed early tonight."

"I'm not going to tell him you're declining his dinner invitation because you're too soft to endure your first day of training. If you want to tell him, go ahead good luck with that, princess."

"Goddamn it alright. Tell him I'll be there."

Dana stepped into the main dining room exactly thirty minutes after she received her summons. She found the new supervisor of North American operations and the man she suspected was the supposedly dead. Detective Trujillo--standing at the head of the elegantly set table for two.

"Señorita Zapata! I'm so pleased that you could join me tonight."

Hernandez reached for Dana's hand, bent over, and kissed it. He straightened his back, looked into her eyes, and smiled.

Those eyes! So blue! Women probably cream their panties just looking at him. "Please, have a seat."

"Thank you," she said.

Hernandez pulled Dana's chair out, waited until she was seated, and then took his place at the head of the table.

"I'm not sure why you requested my presence, but thank you for the honour," Dana said.

"That shouldn't be so difficult to understand. With Señor Las Casas attending business in the capital, I have a rare evening to myself. Is it any surprise that I would prefer the company of a beautiful woman to the brutes in this complex?"

Hernandez waived his hand and a servant approached. He filled two goblets with water, and then retreated.

"I'm sure, Señor Hernandez, that you could obtain the company of any number of beautiful women.

In fact, you could do so without even leaving this house."

"And who would I choose? Maritza? She's nothing but a whore, now Natalia? She belongs to Davis Josefina? Too old and too fat for my taste. The twins? I'm not even sure those beasts are women. Their dicks are probably bigger than mine."

"Señor Hernandez--" "Please, call me Mateo."

"Mateo, I can assure you that Micaela and Na are both women--very beautiful women, in fact." "So you say no matter, I much prefer your company to those two assassins."

"I'm flattered, I guess."

The servant returned with a bottle of rum and a bottle of wine. He poured two snifters of rum, and then uncorked the wine. He reached for the wine goblets, but Hernandez waved him off.

"Not yet," he said.

The servant set the bottle of wine on the table and retreated into the shadows. Hernandez raised his glass of rum.

"To new friends, new relationships, and new business," he said.

"Salúd," Dana responded.

Hernandez drained his glass, but Dana took just a sip.

"Drink up this is very good Jamaican rum I'm planning tosell it in Europe this spring."

Hernandez waved, and the servant reappeared and poured another round minute later another servant appeared and set two salad plates in front of Dana and Hernandez. The first servant returned and poured the wine while Dana nibbled on her salad.

"I watched some of your training today," Hernandez said. "Very impressive" "Um, thank you," Dana replied, "We covered a lot in one day."

"Yes, but you picked everything up very quickly."

"The twins are very capable instructors, and I've always been athletic that had to help."

"No doubt you would agree, I think, that your prior training was focused less on lethality and more on apprehension?"

Dana's heart stopped, she looked up from her plate and saw Hernandez staring at her. "I don't have" she mumbled.

"Come now I recognize Florida Department of Law Enforcement training methods when I see them. I used to be a Miami cop, you know?"

"I'm not."

"Are you City of Miami? Metro-Dade County? Broward Sheriff's Office?"

"I'm not a cop I swear."

"It's OK, Lydia like I said, I used to be a cop."
"Does Las Casas know?"

"About me--yes You--not yet.

Dana's hands were shaking", she wanted to run, but she knew there was nowhere to go.

A servant returned and cleared the salad plates. The other servant refilled the water goblets, topped off the wine glasses, and retreated to the shadows.

"How did he, how did you, how are you still alive?"

Dana rubbed her hands together under the table. She felt a bead of sweat running down her neck. She looked up and saw Hernandez smiling at her. The bastards is enjoying this.

A servant appeared with two plates containing grilled lamb chops, a rice pilaf, and sauteed vegetables. He returned a minute later with a basket of bread and pot of whipped butter.

"I'm an asset," Hernandez said "I make him-money."

"But you're a cop" Dana stared at Hernandez.

"I was a cop" Hernandez took a bite of his food and chewed it very slowly. "Two years ago, I was detective Ivan Trujillo. I was sent undercover to infiltrate the Las Casas organization, I met the late Señor Crespo, gained his trust, and switched sides."

"How did you do that?"

"I turned over an informant Crespo got him to confess, and I killed him. Crespo was impressed."

"Wasn't he suspicious of you?"

"A lot of cops are bad. Do you have any idea how many Miami Police are on our payroll?"

"No."

"Trust me, it wasn't a stretch for him to believe, I switched sides, especially after I started making them crate loads of money."

"How? Why?"

"The 'how' of it was by tightening supply lines and shipping schedules, diversifying investments, and forming strategic alliances with certain governmental officials in various countries where we needed to expand our market share. The 'why' is simple there's too much money in this business to ever go back to law enforcement. I was on the wrong team, I learned that the first month. I was here I could never live the quality of life I'm enjoying now on a meager detective's salary."

"But you were a cop, how did you know about making money for a drug dealer?"

"I majored in accounting in college. My wife is a financial planner, I've learned a few things about making money grow."

"How could you leave your family?"

"It was easy leaving my wife, I think she may have been fucking my partner, I know she wasn't fucking me."

"What about your children?"

"That was more difficult at first, but after being away from them for a few months, I realized that deep down I'm just not a family guy. I needed adventure living at home was suffocating me. Out here, I can breathe again."

"If you're such a financial wizard, then how did Crespo manage to steal so much from Las Casas?"
"He didn't."

Dana choked on her water.

"Excuse me?"

"Crespo didn't steal those millions, I set him up with hundreds of transfers that did nothing more than move money in circles. I forged a few documents, created a few accounts in banks that neither Crespo nor Las Casas had ever heard of, and basically framed him for a theft that never occurred, he did skim around $3-$4 million off the top, but Las Casas would never have killed him over that amount. He would have punished him--maybe even demoted him--but he would not have killed him. His betrayal had to be many times bigger than that to earn him a death sentence."

Dana's jaw hung from her face.

"Why? Why would you do that?"

"He was in my way, I could never rise to this position as long as Crespo was alive."

This man is a monster, They're all monsters, to one degree or another, but he's the worst. What am I doing here? I wish Jorge would return. No, I don't,

I want to go home.

"And now, if you don't mind, it's your turn to answer some questions."

"Um, sure," Dana mumbled. "Let's start with your name."

"You know my name, I'm Lydia Zapata."

"No, I don't know your name, what I do know is that your name is not 'Lydia Zapata'. I have contacts in Miami, and the only record they found of a Lydia Zapata belonged to a nineteen-year-old Guatemalan woman who was deported from Miami two weeks ago. So let's do this again. What's your name?"

"Yuonna Alvarado."

"Good, that wasn't so hard, was it?" "No" Dana whispered.

"What are you doing here?"

"Lydia was bragging about all the money she was going to be making at this fancy boat party. I asked her to hook me up, you know, get me into the party, but she said 'no'. I haven't made any real money in over a month, So I got her drunk, slipped her a sleeping pill, and took her place I didn't know she got deported."

"Where did you get your training?"

"What training? I've worked on and off in bars and clubs for the past three years." "Your police training, I recognised your style from the academy." "I've never had any training, sometimes when I have extra cash I work out at the gym, I spar with some dudes that could be cops. I guess they show me stuff, you know, self-defense moves. They throw me around and feel me up, but they're just after my pussy I know that. They don't know I know."

"I'll check out your story, Dana Lvarado."

"You know, I guess I'm kind of like you, I snuck my way into this world, and now that I'm here, I want to stay. Don't tell Jorge anything that will make him send me back please."

"Like I said, I'll check out your story, and if it holds up, I'll keep your secret."

"Thank you, I think I'd like to go to my room now if you don't mind."

"Good night Dana." Goodnight.

Harris parked his car inside Candee's walled lot and strode inside the building. He waited a second for his eyes to adjust to the dim light. When his vision returned, he waded through the sea of empty tables and chairs standing between the doorway and the back office. Usually, a bouncer would be standing at the hallway entrance leading to the office, but at 10:00, the empty club was still in a relaxed state of operation. The music wasn't booming through the speakers, the dancers were still putting on make-up and skimpy costumes, and the lone bartender was filling the ice bin instead of pouring drinks. The club was technically open, but it was not yet ready for business.

Harris reached for the handle to the office door, but it was locked. He backed up a step and kicked the door with the bottom of his shoe, breaking the lock and splintering the door frame. He stepped inside just as Bryan Jackson reached for a button under the desk.

"Who the fuck are you?" Jackson demanded" Get the hell out of here while you can still walk out on your own two feet."

Harris pulled his gun and pointed it at Jackson's head.

"Don't move hands in the air, now."

Jackson raised his hands above his head. Alexander walked around the desk and stood behind Jackson. He pushed his face down against the hard surface, and then pulled out a pair of handcuffs and attached them to Jackson's wrists.

A large black man wearing jeans and a black t-shirt burst through the open door, Harris pointed his weapon at the bouncer.

"Freeze," he said" Miami Police Department. Get on the ground with your hands behind your head" The bouncer laid on the floor. Harris grabbed Jackson and pulled him to his feet.

"I'm taking this man in for questioning," Harris said." If anyone tries to interfere, you'll be arrested and charged with obstruction of justice."

Harris dragged Jackson through the club and out the door. He threw him in the car, started the engine, and speed off.

"Do you mind telling me what this is all about?" Jackson asked" Or would you rather explain what you're doing to my lawyer?"

"Shut up," Harris said "You'll get a chance to tell your story."

Instead of driving south toward the police station, Harris headed west, he pulled into a warehouse district on the edge of the city and drove into a alley between two crumbling old building. He stopped the car, opened the door, and pulled Jackson from the back seat.

"You were at a party on the sixteenth, out in the Gulf Stream," Alexander said, "Whose boat was it on?"

"Fuck you I wasn't at any party."

Harris slammed his fist into Jackson's stomach "Ungh!"

"You were at the party, we have pictures of you boarding the boat" "Like hell you do."

Harris smashed his fist into Jackson's jaw. Jackson spits blood at Alexander and sneered.

"You don't have any fucking pictures and you know it. Now take me back so that my lawyer can get to work on my police brutality complaint. You can kiss your badge goodbye, asshole."

Harris swung his fist into Jackson's balls. Jackson bent over in pain just as Harris slammed his knee into Jackson's nose. Alexander grabbed the back of Jackson's shirt collar and slammed his head into the car door. With blood streaming from his broken nose, Jackson wobbled on unsteady feet. Alexander punched his stomach, and then pushed him into a warehouse wall.

"In case, you haven't noticed asshole," Alexander snarled at Jackson, "my badge isn't really at the top of my priority list."

Harris pulled his gun from his belt and pressed it against Jackson's head.

"You're going to tell me what I want to know, or I'm going to splatter your brains all over the pavement. Do you understand what I'm telling you?" "I was at the party" Jackson coughed up more blood as he spat out the words.

"Did you see this girl?" Harris pulled a folded sheet of paper from his pocket. It was a picture of Dana that he had printed off his computer.

"I don't know. There were a lot of girls there." Harris punched Jackson in the jaw "Look again."

Jackson stared at the picture "Yeah, I remember her. That whore could really suck a dick, must have swallowed a gallon of jizz. She either sucked or fucked half the guys there that night, what a mouth!"

Harris punched Jackson in the stomach. "Ungh!"

"Where is she? What happened to her after the party?"

"How the fuck should I know? The girls were still there when I left."

"Where's Crespo?"

"Crespo? He is dead." "What? Who? How?"

"Las Casas killed him, or had him killed, I don't know the details, I wasn't there."

"You weren't where?" "Crespo's house in Honduras." "When?"

"A week ago, two weeks maybe, I wasn't there" "How do you know?"

"I don't, actually, all I know is Crespo is dead, and my new partner is a guy Named Hernandez, I've never met him before, Can't tell you what he looks like or anything about him."

Alexander pushed the barrel of his gun against Jackson's temple. His finger rested on the trigger "Where in Honduras?"

"I'm a dead man if I tell you that "You're a dead man if you don't". You've got time to run from them. You've got three seconds left with "Roatán" "Where?"

"Roatán is an island Crespo when he was alive, he controlled everything there."

Beads of sweat dotted Harris' forehead. The back of his shirt and his underarms were soaked, Jackson's blood streaked the sleeves and front panels.

"I should blow your god damned head off."

"What the fuck did I ever do to you? don't tell me you are tapping that whore?"

Harris swung his arm wide, sweeping arc, slamming the handle of the gun against the side of Jackson's skul. Jackson fell to the ground, unconscious blood was streaming from his nose and the side of his head. Harris removed the cuffs, rolled Jackson onto his stomach, and left him behind a dumpster. He got back into his car and spead off.

A security camera mounted on the side of the building, tracked his car until it rounded the corner, and then the small red light on top of the camera flickered out.

Dana spent the next two days training with the twins. She tried to focus her attention and absorb everything they could teach her about eliminating a threat as quietly and efficiently as possible. She spent extra hours handling and firing the various automatic weapons at her disposal, as well as various blades, truncheons, and even a garrote. Despite her best efforts to unlearn her prior training--training that was geared more toward subduing and capturing a perpetrator rather than terminating a potential threat, she found herself resorting to the techniques she had spent the better part of the summer learning to master. Her distraction, she realized, stemmed from the fact that she was constantly looking over her shoulder for any sign of Hernandez.

She didn't know what to do about Hernandez. The fact that he was still alive meant that everything the department thought they knew about Crespo and Las Casas was wrong. She didn't know if Hernandez was still undercover, or if he had turned. Hell, I don't know if I'm still undercover or if I've turned. All I know for sure is that he's my biggest threat and potentially my only ally.

Las Casas returned from Tegucigalpa in the evening following Dana's third day of training. She was in the yacht's Jacuzzi nursing her aching body when the helicopter landed in the field behind the house. Dana got out of the hot tub, showered, and waited for Las Casas to join her in the stateroom.

It was two hours later when the door opened and Las Casas entered the room, Dana was laying naked on top of the bed, sound asleep Las Casas undressed in the dark and crawled into bed beside her.

CHAPTER 4

Dana awoke to Las Casas' hands, pawing her breasts, and his face nuzzling her neck.

"Mmmm," she purred, "It's about time you came home."

"This isn't my home," he corrected, "but we will be going there shortly."

Dana reached for his cock, which was already erect. She steered the head toward her pussy and rubbed the tip against her lower lips.

"Did you miss me?" she cooed.

"More than you can imagine, my lady" "Show me," she said.

Dana placed the tip of his cock against her moist opening and pushed her cheeks backward.

"Not so fast," he said "Before I make love to my lady, I'm going to fuck my whore."

Las Casas grabbed a fistful of Dana's hair and pulled her head to his crotch.

"You're going to show me how much you missed my presence," he snarled.

Dana parted her lips to accept his erect cock teeth, and all the way to the back of her throat.

Las Casas thrust his manhood into Dana's mouth, past her, using her hair to control her movements, he bobbed her head up and down on his swollen shaft. Dana was used to the rough treatment, but she had been hoping for a repeat of their last night together. She didn't know what the return of his rougher treatment signified, but it worried her. I've got no choice but to give him what he wants.

Saliva flowed out of Dana's mouth. It ran down the length of Las Casas' shaft, soaking his balls and making a swamp in the bed sheet, beneath his ass. Dana's scalp was burning and she was constantly fighting her gag reflex. She tasted his pre-cum sooner than expected, and realized that Las Casas probably hadn't cum since leaving two days ago, I was sure he would have visited a whore or three while he was gone. Maybe he does have feelings for me?

A familiar feeling washed over Dana. Her body shuddered involuntarily, and then her face felt warm. She pushed all thoughts out of her mind save for one: pleasing her man in the way he wanted to be pleased. She cupped his balls with one hand and circled the base of his shaft with the other. She increased the speed of her head movement. His hand clutching her hair was unnecessary. She was doing everything she could to help him cum.

Dana bobbed her head up and down on Las

Casas 's erect cock. She squeezed his balls and stroked the base of his thick shaft. She ignored the pain in her jaws, she ignored her gag reflex, and the tugging on her scalp. She tasted more of his precum and knew he was close to coming.

"Ye!" Las Casas screamed "Puta chingada! Chupalo!"

Dana felt his balls contract, She increased the speed of her hand on his cock even as she felt it swelling in her fingers. She opened her mouth as wide as possible and swallowed his entire shaft.

"Ungh! DȘos mȘo!"

Las Casas' cock throbbed. The first jet of cum rushed up his shaft and splashed against the back of Dana's throat. She swallowed as much of the cream as she could, but the second blast filled her mouth and escaped her lips before she gulped a second time. She swallowed again and again, but the juice was flowing faster than her throat could open and close Saliva and semen ran out of her mouth and soaked his balls before pooling in the sheet between his thighs.

"Enough! Stop! No more!" Las Casa pushed Dana's head away from his cock "That was incredible You're mmmmmmmmmm"

Dana swallowed the cum that was in her mouth and swiped her tongue across her chin to catch the overflow. She laid her head on Las Casas chest and felt his heart pounding in her ear. Her hand rested on his thigh, inches from his shrinking cock.

Ten minutes later, when his heart was once again beating its normal rhythm, Dana turned to face Las Casas. She reached for his cock and stroked it.

"I can see that you missed your whore, but what about your lady?"

"My sweet angel," he answered, "I will spend the rest of this night and all of tomorrow showing her how much she was missed."

Dana turned to kiss him, but Las Casas started to turn away. Fuck it. I'm not brushing my teeth now. She placed both hands on the sides of his head and lowered his mouth to hers.

"Your lady wants a kiss," she whispered, "and she isn't going to wait another second."

Dana pressed her mouth against Las Casas' lips. He hesitated for a second, and then parted his mouth to accept her probing tongue. His pink organ met hers and then ventured into her mouth. He wrapped his arms around her and squeezed her while his tongue explored the insides of her cheeks.

Las Casas rolled Dana onto her back. She opened her thighs and drew her knees up to her chest. She looked into his dark eyes with an urgency that she knew would threaten her self-control. She was past caring.

"Your lady wants you," she moaned "She needs to get fucked."

Las Casas rubbed the tip between her lips and over her clit. When the head felt slippery enough, he placed it against her opening and pushed. Her flesh parted to receive him. She was hot and wet and more than willing. He pushed until he was buried inside her.

"Oh, I've missed you these past three days," she said.

"And I've missed you. Every night was agony without you."

"Fuck me, Fuck your lady, Fuck your lady like you would fuck your whore."

"If I fuck my lady like I fuck my whore, will she still be my lady?"

"I think the better question is if you don't fuck your lady like your whore, will she still be yours?"
"That is a question to which I hope I never want to know the answer."

Dana and Las Casas slept into the early afternoon. They had fucked the previous night until after midnight, slept for an hour, but then Las Casas awoke and they fucked again. They slept until dawn- and Dana awoke when the first sliver of sunlight leaked through the stateroom windows. She aroused Las Casas and they fucked once more, before rolling over and sleeping until a servant brought them lunch a little after 1:00 pm.

They emerged from the boat late in the afternoon. The twins greeted them in the main room of the house. The four settled into plush chairs while a servant poured coffee into small cups. The servant returned moments later with a large pitcher of ice water. Davis entered the room and took a seat closer to the door.

"Where's Mateo?" Las Casas asked.

"He left this morning for Mexico City," Davis answered, "Said he had to look into some investment opportunities, and other matters. He could be back tomorrow night possibly another day or two if everything goes well."

"Very well, I'll get his report when he returns Franklin, have you had any success decrypting the rest of Crespo's files?"

"Yes Sir. He used some archaic code that he must have obtained from the Turks or Lebanese and almost through the last of it."

"And? any traces of where to find the rest of my money?"

"I would want to let Hernandez explain what we've found, It's difficult for me to interpret the meaning of all those transactions. There were something going on in Africa that I don't fully understand."

"I see very well, I'll talk to him when he gets back. You're excused."

"Thank you boss, Davis stood up and headed for the door.

"One more thing, Franklin." Davis stopped at the doorway. "How is Natalia?"

"She's doing better boss, The doctor says it will be another week before she's fully detoxified Heroin, that's some Nasty stuff."

"How is she coping with the loss of Requilio?"
"She's not missing him as much as you might expect, I'm sure of that."

"Excellent, she deserves an honourable man like you, after being married to that ratžn. Close the door on your way out."

Davis left the room.

Las Casas turned his gaze toward the twins.

"Ana, how is the training of our newest asset coming along?"

Dana blushed at the reference to herself as an "asset.

"She's proceeding remarkably well," Ana answered."

"I would almost believe that she had some training before you acquired her."

"I disagree," Micaela interrupted. "With the exception of a handgun, she had no familiarity with any firearms, she didn't know how to use a knife, her skill with a truncheon was laughable. She knew some self-defense moves, but she lacked any kind of lethality in hand-to-hand combat few lessons, maybe, but serious training. The average Havana street kid would have gutted her and left her for dead."

"No matter, what I want to know is, how is she progressing?"

"Very well," Ana answered.

"She's trainable," Micaela interjected "She learns quickly, she has excellent balance and she's in great physical condition, as I'm sure you know better than us."

Dana blushed. The twins giggled and Las Casas stared at Micaela for three seconds before the corners of his mouth softened into a slight smile.

"Yes, she is quite a specimen," Las Casas finally said.

"I'm right here" Dana waved "Hello."

"How long before she's ready?" Las Casas asked. "Ready for what?" Dana interrupted.

"At least two more weeks," Micaela answered. "Her superb conditioning helps us accelerate her training, but she still has a lot to learn about weapons, especially automatic weapons."

"She's putting in extra time, and that is helping immensely," Ana added "Although missing today's sessions was a bit of a setback."

"That couldn't be helped," Las Casas said," I was in need of her other skills."

Dana's face flushed crimson. She stood up and looked at all three of them.

"Are you just going to continue talking about me like I'm not even here? What am I being trained for?" Las Casas finished sipping his cafecito and set down his cup. He lifted his glass, took a long drink of water, and then looked into Dana's eyes. "You're going to be my master assassin."

Dana approached her training with even greater diligence over the next three days. She was horrified at the thought of becoming an assassin, but she realised that by committing to a definite role in the organization, her value to Las Casas increased. Maximizing her value was the key to improving her chances of survival. Even if his feelings for her were genuine --and she was starting to believe that they were--she knew that she could easily be replaced if he had any reason to think of her again as just another whore. But becoming a vital cog in his enterprise would make her harder to supplant. Her short-term goal, therefore, was to become "vital."

Her biggest obstacle was Hernandez. He alone knew that she was lying about her past. Even worse, he had the resources and the wherewithal to discover the true reason she was on board in Las Casas' yacht three weeks earlier. He was also her biggest potential allied. His background was the most similar to hers. Together, the two of them could bring down the entire organization Strangely, that thought held very little appeal to her.

Harris made two stops on his way to the airport.

The first was at a gun shop. After showing the salesman his concealed weapon permit, Alexander purchased a Glock of 20 10mm handgun, a stainless steel travel case, and 200 rounds of ammunition.

His next stop was at the bank. Harris took out $25,000 in cash from his personal accounts, and then transferred the remaining balance into a little used joint account he held with his mother.

He left his car in the long term garage at the airport. He was planning to be back in twenty-four hours, but there were too many variables, he could not control going up against a major drug cartel on their home turf--all by himself--sounded like a suicide plan. He thought of enlisting Zac's assistance- after all, he was the bastard who got him into this mess--but he no longer trusted him. That thought saddened him a little, but he pushed it out of his mind once he shut off the car engine. He would have plenty of time for regrets on the return trip.

Harris was prepared for a lengthy delay at the airline counter. He had never before flown with a weapon in his luggage, but everyone he talked to told him it would be a pain in the ass. That was an understatement. No one he talked to had ever flown internationally.

By the time he finished the paperwork, met with Honduran officials, was searched, strip-searched, and interviewed by TS, F, and FBI agents, his plane had already taxied onto the runway, been cleared for take off, and left MI Harris' only alternative was to book a seat on the next available flight, which was scheduled for departure twenty-four hours later.

Hernandez returned after dinner on the third evening, Las Casas met with him behind closed doors for over three hours, Dana waited nervously. She was anxious to find out if Hernandez had uncovered her deception, but she was fatigued from her day long training sessions. Eventually, sleep overcame her. At 2:00 am, Las Casas crawled into bed with Dana. He kissed her cheeks and forehead until she stirred.

When she realised he was there, she pressed her lips to his and returned his kisses. Her anxiety diminished the longer Las Casas kissed her. He wouldn't be kissing me if I were about to die Right?

"I'm leaving in the morning," Las Casas said

"Where are you going?"

"Barranquilla I'm taking Maritza and Josefina." "Why?"

"It's time for Maritza to go to work."

"What about Josefina? She's a little old to work in a whorehouse, isn't she?"

"Correct I think I'll put her to work on a coca farm. That way, I'll never have to see her or hear her mouth again."

"Aren't you worried that she'll find sympathizers? She could escape."

"Not a problem, I've already replaced everyone who was loyal to Crespo. She'll be surrounded by his rivals I think they'll keep her in line."

"How are you getting there? are you taking the yacht?"

"No I'll take the helicopter, I can get there in one day if we don't run into bad weather. It would take three days by boat."

"Isn't that kind of far? What's the range of that chopper?"

"We'll have to stop three times to refuel: Nicaragua, Costa Rica, and Panama. Still, I'd rather get there in one long day than spend three days at sea with Crespo's women."

"Since you put it that way, I think I prefer that you take the chopper, also I couldn't bear the thought of you spending your nights at sea with Josefina."

"You have nothing to worry about."

"But I do worry, you really seemed to enjoy fucking her fat ass."

"I was doing it for effect, only."

"She seemed to enjoy it, are you sure you don't want to hit it one more time before she's gone?" "The only ass I want to fuck right now is yours."

"That's what you say, but words are meaningless, I need to be convinced."

"Then allow me to persuade you."

Las Casas rolled Dana onto her stomach. He lifted her ass into the air and spit on her asshole. He licked it until she was relaxed, and then spit on it again. He placed the head of his erect cock against her anus and pushed. The saliva provided just enough lubrication, enabling him to force the head of his cock inside of her.

"Is that all you've got?" Dana teased "I'll bet you'd give Josefina more than you're giving me."

"I could shove a baseball bat up Josefina's ass with little difficulty. Your's is a little more challenging."

"Just a little bit? are you calling me easy?"

Las Casas withdrew his cock, spit one more time on Dana's sphincter, and then replaced the tip of his cock in her anus. He pushed until the head popped through, pulled back, and pushed again an inch of shaft disappeared between her cheeks. He pulled back and pushed again and again until his cock was buried inside her.

"Ungh!" Dana grunted "I have to say that you do make a compelling argument."

Las Casas pulled back and then thrust forward again.

"Ungh! I am ungh starting to see your point."

Las Casas thrust into her with the full length of his cock.

"That's ungh conclusive ungh proof."

Las Casas leaned forward and pushed her head into the bed. He held her down and thrust in out of her asshole with increasing forcefulness.

"Ungh! OK, I'm convinced."

"Ungh! Ungh!" Las Casas grunted "I'mahhhhhhhh!"

Las Casas exploded inside her ass. He thrust several times, pumping jet after jet of semen into her rectum. He slowed his pace, shortened his stroke, and then collapsed on top of Dana's prone body. He sounded asleep within seconds.

Dana and Las Casas arose before dawn. They showered, dressed, and then enjoyed an early breakfast on the deck of the yacht. As soon as the dishes were cleared, Las Casas convened a meeting with Hernandez, Davis, and Dana in the entertainment salon.

Hernandez and Las Casas took the overstuffed lounge chairs Davis paced on perimeter of the room. Dana avoided making eye contact with Hernandez. She sat on the sofa where she had previously enjoyed her first lesbian experience and where General Torres subsequently ravaged her asshole. The first memory provoked a hint of a smile, but it disappeared when she recalled her treatment at the hands of the aged anal rapist.

"Franklin," Las Casas called "Sit down We're about to begin."

"I'm sorry, boss, but I'm feeling a little under the weather today," Davis answered "This meeting was not on my calendar."

"You'll be fine, I'm sure. Get yourself something to drink and join us, your input in these matters are important."

"Thank you boss, I'll be there in a second." Davis disappeared behind the bar.

"Gentlemen --and Lydia--as you know, I'll be departing as soon as the chopper is ready," Las Casas announced, "Before I go, updates please, how did things go in Mexico City?"

"We have competition," Hernandez answered in a solemn tone "The Saltillo Cartel has expanded its influence in the Federal District, I have evidence that certain officials who we bought and paid for are also collecting payments from Saltillo."

"Who?"

"Cástanon, definitely, and either Ruşz or Obregžn, I'm not sure which one, yet and maybe Peralta, also."

"Peralta, Peralta do you mean Pilar?" "Yes, the mayor's assistant."

"Are you sure?"

"Not yet, but she was extremely nervous when I talked to her. She kept looking over her shoulder, like she thought she was being watched. Her answers touched upon the truth, but were more evasive than revealing. I could tell she was hiding something."

"What do you recommend?"

"We need to make a statement."

"My thought exactly, How long before we need to act?"

"It depends on the target right now, if it's Cástanon, I'll need more time to develop a profile if it's RuŞz or Obregžn Peralta--that one's especially tricky. It depends on how much help Davis can give me in collecting and analysing the data."

"The selection can wait until I return. We're not quite ready to deploy our asset, so there's no need to rush into a decision."

"Gentleman," Davis interrupted, "We have another problem."

All heads turned toward Davis, who was standing behind the bar holding a small metal device between his fingers. Dana felt a pain in her chest as her heart nearly stopped. Fuck! I should have thrown that thing away!

"I found this bug attached to a shelf," Davis said "The battery is dead, but someone placed it here recently."

Hernandez looked at Dana, and then turned toward Davis.

"How recently?" Las Casas demanded.

"Three to four weeks ago."

"Torres!" Las Casas snarled, "I'll kill the bastard" "Are you sure it was him?" Hernandez asked.

"It had to be him, the last time this room was swept for electronics was the day before the party. He's the only outsider who's been in here since then, his aides didn't even enter the room."

"I don't know," Hernandez said "He's been loyal for years, he has no reason to turn."

"Apparently, he does maybe he thinks he can regain his influence with Castro or supplement his retirement by selling us out. Maybe Saltillo made him a better offer. Find out before I return, Mateo Start with the twins, they'll know what Hernandez was planning. If Saltillo is behind this, we'll need to make our move, I want a full report as soon as I get back."

"Next week?"

"No, tomorrow night, I'm cuttin my trip short" Las Casas stormed out of the room without saying goodbye to Dana. She was less offended by that omission than she would have expected at the time, she was too paralyzed to notice. You landed in Roatán a few minutes past noon customs, it was almost 2:00 in the afternoon.

By the time, he retrieved his luggage and cleared soon as his bags were in hand, he stopped in a restroom. He opened his suitcases, removed his gun and the ammunition, and loaded the magazine. He tucked the gun into his pants, pulled his shirt over his waistline, and headed for the car rental counter. The Glock 20 made a noticeable bulge in his clothing, so he had to carry the suitcase in front of him to hide it from prying eyes.

Dana spent the morning locked in her stateroom

on the yacht Hernandez placed a guard outside the doorway, and another near the staircase, a third guard was stationed on the yacht's rear deck, and a fourth guard patrolled the dock. Hernandez told her they were there for her protection, but Dana was sure they were meant to keep her from escaping.

In the early afternoon, Dana heard a knock on the stateroom door. She grabbed a small pocket knife and held it behind her back.

"Come in," she said man she did not know entered the room. He was wearing an automatic rifle on his shoulder.

"Señor Hernandez will see you," the guard said in a disinterested monotone.

"Tell him I'm busy, I'll meet with him in thirty minutes."

"He wants to see you now."

Dana detected a note of menace in his voice that was not present a second ago. She did not know Hernandez' intentions, but based on the messenger's comportment, she guessed that they were not solicitous. Either way, she reminded herself, he was dangerous.

"Who do you work for, Hernandez or Las Casas?" Dana demanded.

"Two weeks ago, I worked for Crespo but you killed him. Now, I just do what I'm told."

"And I'm telling you, I will meet with Hernandez in thirty minutes."

"Señora, some days I get orders from Señor Jorge, and some days they come from Señor Mateo. No one has ever told me that I am to take orders from you. No one, now let's go."

The man grabbed Dana by the wrist and pulled her out of the room. Dana saw no advantage to fighting with the man, so she let him herd her off the boat and into the house. She was brought to the main room, where Hernandez was waiting for her. Hernandez's shirt was ripped in two places, his ear was torn and bleeding, and his nose was swollen and bloodied. When Dana got close enough, she could see that it was broken. So much for his beautiful face. "Thank you for joining me," he said "I need to discuss some things with you, are you hungry?"

Hernandez waved his arm in the direction of the table, where two places were set with a tray of grilled meats and sausages on the table, along with a basket of bread and a wedge of cheese.

Dana had not eaten all day, but her stomach was too upset to send a hunger signal to her brain. She tried her best not to tremble when Hernandez took her hand and led her to the table. She took a seat and sat quietly while a servant carved some meats and cheese and placed them on her plate.

"I'm going to need your help," Hernandez said.

"Jorge is returning tonight, and he wants answers when he arrives."

"Tonight? I thought he wouldn't be back until tomorrow."

"This situation is too urgent, he's leaving Crespo's women at his Costa Rican estate and turning back."

"What do you want from me?"

"You've spent more time with the twins than anyone I want you to interrogate Na. I've been working on Micaela all day, but so far she hasn't given up anything useful."

"Is that what happened to your nose?"

"Yes but don't worry, that bitch is in far worse shape. She has to be close to breaking, but if she doesn't survive long enough to talk, I'll need you to get the information out of her sister. We don't have much time."

"I've never, alright I'll do it."

"If you succeed, I'm sure Jorge will be extremely pleased. But if you fail, the focus of this investigation may shift to other suspects."

Dana winced, she knew he was referring to her, "I won't fail I promise."

"Make sure you don't, I have Micaela in the cellar Na is in Maritza's old bedrooms soon as you find out something, come get me."

"I will."

Climbing the stairs to the second floor, Dana walked with a purposeful stride that belied her terror. She noted one guard at the bottom of the staircase, another at the top of the stairs, and one outside the room that belonged to Maritza before serving as Na's cell. She knew all eyes were watching her, but the men did not seem to regard her with suspicion. Instead, some of the men were avoiding eye contact with her, as though they were ones with something to hide. It seems that everyone is a little on edge everyone except for Hernandez.

Dana walked up to the guard standing outside the bedroom doorway. Like the others, he too looked away when she looked directly at him.

"Señor Hernandez sent me to interrogate the prisoner," she said.

"He told me to be expecting you" The man reached into his pocket for the key. He unlocked the door but did not open it.

"What is your name?" "Raúl."

"Raúl, lock this door behind me and do not let anyone else enter, unless it is Señor Las Casas or Señor Hernandez. Do you understand?"

"Yes, Señora."

Dana opened the door and stepped inside the room. She pulled the door shut behind herself second later, she heard the lock click shut as soon as she turned toward the wrought iron bed, Dana saw the reason why the men were so nervous. Na was lying on the bed, naked. Her wrists were tied to her ankles with coarse ropes and her legs were splayed at almost a 180 degree angle. Her arms were fastened to the headboard of the old iron bed with lengths of rope and additional lengths were used to attach her legs to the footboard. She was also gagged and blindfolded. The sheets were soaked in sweat and semen, especially in the area beneath her crotch.

Whoever bound Na was an expert in rope play. There was an elegance and symmetry to her display that was artistic and--in a perverse way--almost beautiful. She was utterly immobilized, and she was definitely in pain. Only someone in peak physical condition and with the flexibility of a gymnast could have survived the process by which she ended up in that position.

Dana removed the gag from Na's mouth, she left the blindfold in place.

"What do you fuckers want now?" Na spat "If you put a dick in my mouth, I swear I'll bite it off." "Nobody's going to put a dick in your mouth,"

Dana said,

"You? What do you want? Where's my sister?" "Hernandez sent me to interrogate you he's interrogating Micaela."

"What is this about? Take this blindfold off me" "In time first, answer some questions for me." "What do you want? I don't know anything Micaela doesn't know anything. We haven't done anything except follow orders."

"Who has questioned you already?"

"No one, you're the first person to talk to me since I was brought in here and tied to this bed."

"Who tortured you?"

"Do you mean who violated me? Just about everyone, I think I lost count after the fifth one climbed on top of me. Ten, twelve, fifteen, I'm not sure, does it matter?"

"No, not really."

"But that's all they've done, so far. No one has asked me anything, and they haven't physically tortured me or even threatened me."

"Listen to me very carefully, Na there is video surveillance in this room, but they never installed audio equipment. We're probably being watched, so I'm going to have to act like I'm questioning you-- aggressively questioning you but they can't hear us, so we'll be able to talk, do you understand?"

"Yes."

"I'm going to remove your blindfold."

Dana stood at the head of the bed. She pulled the small knife out of her pocket and cut away the knotted rag covering Na's eyes.

"Now untie me," Na pleaded.

"I'm sorry, but I can't do that yet, I'm working on a plan, but until we're ready to act on it, you're going to have to remain tied up once I free you, we'll have to move very quickly."

"Wonderful well, you've always wanted to know what my pussy looked like are you enjoying the view?"

"Shut up, Na I'm not enjoying this, and I'm afraid you're not going to like what I have to tell you next" "What's that?"

"I'm going to have to beat you a little, anyone watching has to believe that I'm interrogating you." "Go ahead it's not like you could hurt me."

Dana realized that she should have stopped at the armory, but the only implement she brought that could be classified as a weapon was the small pocket knife she picked up on the yacht. It didn't make much of an impression. She looked around the room for inspiration, but saw nothing of use. She paced the perimeter of the room, pausing at the window to look out onto the grounds. Pushing the curtains aside, she peered out the window and let her mind wander. She attempted to gauge the hour based upon the angle and length of the shadows forming along the tree line between two and three? Little past three, maybe? She stepped away from the window and let the curtain fall into place. Suddenly, she had an idea.

Dana grabbed the curtain and yanked it downward. The screws anchoring the rod to the wall pulled loose and bent. She reached above her head to full extension and grabbed the curtain at its highest point. She lifted her feet off the ground and let the curtain support her entire weight. The rod ripped from the wall as she crashed to the floor. She stood up and grabbed the other curtain, pulling the rod entirely free after tearing the curtain rod off the wall, Dana pulled the two pieces apart. She placed the longer piece near the door the bed frame grasping the shorter section, she whipped it back and forth and then slammed against it. The clanging noise of the metal-on-metal impact reverberated throughout the room.

"OK, bitch, now you're going to talk," Dana said "Make sure you hit me on the fleshy part of my thighs," Na said, "That rod is going to break bones if you miss."

"I'm not planning to hit you that hard." "Then you're going to get us killed."

Dana brought the rod down on Na's left thigh, striking her midway between her knee and her crotch.

"Owwww!"

"Was that too hard?"

"Just hard enough." Tears streamed down Na's face and welt appeared on her thigh.

"Your sister is downstairs, in the cellar Hernandez has been interrogating her all day."

"Torturing her, you mean we don't have much time, Lydia." "I know."

"Hit me again." "Are you ready?"

"Yes, damn it do it."

Dana hit Na's right thigh, just above the knee "Owwww! Fuck!" "Are you OK?"

"Yes, goddamn you. That was close, you almost hit my knee."

"I'm sorry" welt appeared a few inches above Na's right knee.

"If you break my leg, I won't be much help to you or Micaela" "I said I'm sorry."

"Just be more careful, next time."

"OK."

"Where are the guards?"

"There's one outside the door. There's another at the top of the stairs, and another at the bottom of the stairs. I haven't been in the cellar, so I don't know what we'll find when we go downstairs."

"Hit me again."

"No."

"It's alright Do it."

"I'm afraid I'll break something." "Then twist my nipples."

"Are you serious?"

"You have to put on a show for whomever is watching" "I know, but ..."

"Just do it."

Dana put down the rod and leaned over Na's bound body. The brunette woman's brown nipples were standing at attention on her small, tanned breasts. Dana closed her fingers around each nipple and pinched.

"Is that the best you can do?" Na taunted "It feels like you're trying to turn me on. We don't have time to make love."

Dana clenched her teeth and turned her hands in opposite directions.

"You're going to get us killed if they think you're trying to seduce me, Pinch Harder."

Dana pressed her thumbs against her forefingers and squeezed the little brown nubs. She twisted her wrists from side-to-side, applying more and more pressure until she feared she was going to pull Na's nipples right off her tits. When Dana looked down, she saw tears streaming from Na's eyes.

"Owwww! Fuck fuck fuck! Damn you!" "I'm sorry."

"Shut up here's the plan, you're going to excuse yourself and go to the surveillance room, it's right next door. You're going to take out anyone in that room, and then come back. You'll lure the guard in here, and then take him out. You'll release me, and then we'll head for the armory. We're going to have to take out anyone between the armoury and the cellar, starting with the guards at either end of the stairs Got it?"

"Na--I don't know if I can do that."

"What do you mean you don't know? We were training you to be an assassin. Now is your chance to prove that we weren't wasting our time."

"I don't know if I'm ready."

"You don't have a choice, either you're ready, or we're dead. Those are the options."

"You're right, I don't have any choice." "Hit me one more time before you go." "Are you sure?"

"Just do it."

Dana picked up the rod and swung it at Na's right thigh. Her blow struck dead centre between Na's knee and crotch.

"Owwwwwww! Fuck I hate you fucking goddamn whore."

Dana walked across the room and knocked. The guard unlocked the door and cracked it open.

"I'm coming out for a minute" She pulled the door open and stepped out before the guard could stop her. She walked to the next door and knocked. "I don't think you can go in there," Raúl said as he stepped toward Dana "you telling me how to do my job?" Dana snarled.

"No, Señora" Raúl retreated to his post.

The door to the computer room opened, and Dana pushed her way through sealed the entrance behind her.

Hernandez pulled up an old wooden stool he found in the corner of the cellar. The hydraulic door closer.

He sipped eighteen year old single malt scotch from a crystal tumbler, which he set on the stool between swallows.

In the centre of the room, Micaela was trussed like an animal. Her wrists and ankles were bound together behind her back. Her nude body was hanging at shoulder level from a heavy beam that ran the length of the room, and from which a half-dozen other h o o k s and c h a i n s w e r e mounted. Small weights hung from chains clamped to her nipples. Her body was covered with red welts and purple bruises. Whip marks criss-crossed her back, butt and thighs. She bled from her nose and mouth. Hernandez lit a cigar and blew a cloud of smoke in her face. "Your sister has already admitted that the two of you planted the bug" Hernandez paused to take another long draw on his cigar. He blew the smoke in her direction and continued. "It was a rather painful confession for her to make, but it was the last thing she said before passing out."

"If you got what you wanted, then why are you still interrogating me?"

"That was helpful, but it wasn't enough. What I want to know is, why? What is Torres up to? Who is he working with? Is Castro giving him orders? Or is someone else paying him?"

"I already told you" Micaela coughed up a mouthful of blood which she spat on the floor "We didn't do it El General isn't up to anything."

"Yes, that is what you keep saying. But your twin is telling us a different story. She says that you planted the bug, and that you were the one working with Torres this point, I don't know who to believe. One thing I do know, however, is that I will get the truth out of you. One of you is going to tell me everything I want to know. The other will be dead." "Go to hell, mentiroso, and take your lies with you. If you kill either of us, the other will cut off your balls and feed them to you for your last meal."

Hernandez finished his scotch and then threw the crystal tumbler against a brick wall. Glass exploded in all directions. He reached between Micaela's legs, pinched her clit between his thumb, and finger, and squeezed with all his strength.

"Then I'll just have to kill both of you," he snarled.

The surveillance room contained two large tables filled with computer monitors, an array of servers mounted in a walk-in closet, several printers, and various devices Dana did not recognize. The room was cooled to an uncomfortably low temperature.

There was one armed man in the room. He returned to his seat in front of the monitors.

"Are you watching the interrogation next door?" Dana asked.

"Yes," the man answered, "I'm monitoring all the cameras"

"Where's Davis?"

"Señor Hernandez sent him into town to pick up a shipment of some new equipment. He was pissed when he found it, the audio still wasn't working next door. Davis won't be back for several hours."

"I need to see what happened before I entered the room. I think I missed something important. Can you go back to the point when that puta was first brought in?"

"Sure, just give me a minute."

The man sat at a keyboard and start tapping keys Dana stood behind him while he pulled up the video and stopped it at various points.

"Almost there," he said.

He tapped a few more keys and then stopped as four men dragged Na's hooded body into the room.

"This is it."

"Can you burn this part on to a DVD for me?" she asked.

"Sure, just give me one minute."

Dana circled behind the man while he tore open a package of discs. When he bent over to insert a disc into a drive, she swung the rod with all of her strength. The solid iron finial struck him in the head, smashing his skull. He fell out of his chair as a pool of blood spread out on the floor. Dana wiped the rod on the dead man's shirt. She went around the room and pulled the plug on every device before heading for the door. I can't believe I just killed a man in cold blood. What have I become?

Raúl was standing at his post outside Maritza's room when Dana approached.

"Open the door," she said, "and follow me."

"I don't think so Señor Hernandez ordered me to wait here" "Did he tell you to ignore my orders?"

"No, Señora."

"Listen, Raúl. I need someone with a big fat cock to fuck that puta in the ass while I ram this rod down her throat. Can you help me with that, or should I find someone else? Someone who isn't a faggot?"

"I'm not a fag."

"Then follow me."

Raúl unlocked the door, Dana pushed it open and walked in, with Raúl trailing a step behind. She walked over to the bed and pointed.

"Go ahead, Raúl, she's all yours. Fuck her as hard and as deep and as rough as you like but only in her ass. If you put it in her pussy, the whore might enjoy it. That won't help me get the answers I'm looking for."

"No, please, no more," Na sobbed "Please don't rape my ass again. Not you, too please, Raúl."

"Be a man, Raúl either fuck this whore's ass, or I'll find someone else who will."

Raúl set his K-47 next to the bed. He pulled his pants down to his knees and climbed over the ropes securing Na's legs to the footboard. He knelt in front of her splayed thighs and stroked his cock. When it was erect, he placed the head against Na's gaping asshole and pushed.

"No, no, no," Na cried "He's too big I can't take it, his cock is too big."

"Shut up whore I told you that if you didn't tell me what I wanted to know, then Raúl's big cock in your ass would make you talk."

Raúl pumped back and forth, forcing more and more of his shaft into Na's ass. When he was all the way in, he leaned forward and placed his hands on Na's waist Using her body for leverage, he pumped in and out of her with more speed.

Dana stood near the headboard. She jabbed Na in the face with the finial, and then pushed it against her mouth.

"Tell me what I want to know," Dana demanded." If you don't, Raúl will destroy your asshole." "Oh god, he's so big. He's ripping my asshole make him stop."

"Fuck her harder, Raúl! Shred this whore's ass! Make her talk!"

Raúl was close to cumming. He closed his eyes and thrust in and out, faster and faster. He wanted to hold out, to prolong the pleasure, but the sensations were too much. His body spasmed, and then he fell forward, collapsing on top of Na. Warm blood rushed from his skull and covered Na's heaving torso. Dana stood behind him, wielding her curtain rod.

"Get him off me Hurry."

Dana pushed Raúl to the floor. She pulled out her pocket knife and started cutting through the ropes immobilising Na.

"Don't you have anything bigger than that?" Na asked.

"Hold on."

Dana jumped off the bed and searched Raúl's body. She found a knife tucked into his belt, and another one hidden in his boot. She cut Na's hands free and then gave her one of the knives.

It took nearly ten minutes to cut through all the knots. Na tried to stand once she was free of the ropes, but her legs refused to cooperate.

"Are you OK?" Dana asked. "Give me a second."

Na used a pillow case to wipe Raúl's blood from her body after five minutes of alternately tensing and relaxing her muscles, she was able to stand. She went to a closet and searched through Maritza's clothes. She picked a tank top and a pair of slacks that were close to her size. The only shoes she found were high heels, but she did come across a pair of bedroom slippers. She put them on, grabbed Raúl's gun, and headed for the door.

"You lead," Na said "Our timing has to be precise One slip up, and we're all dead." Dana opened the door and walked out into the hallway. When she reached the stairs, she stopped and told the guard that she was heading to the kitchen for a pitcher of water. The guard gave her a disinterested nod and looked away. Without looking back, she sauntered down the wide, open staircase. The downstairs guard looked up at her when her shoe first touched the stair, and then looked away as she descended the staircase. With her left hand gliding across the banister, Dana slipped her right hand under her shirt and grasped the knife tucked uncomfortably into the waistband of her slacks. I hope Na is in place. If she's not, then I'm as good as dead. When she was two steps from the bottom, Dana pulled out the knife, took another step so that she was directly behind the guard, and sliced his neck from ear to ear. The guard dropped to the floor as blood gushed from his wound.

Dana turned and looked up to the top of the stairs. The other guard was crumpled in a bloody heap. Na silently stepped around his body and joined Dana at the bottom of the staircase.

Alexander drove into the central business district and searched for a realtor. He stopped at the first office he found. He parked his rental car in front of the building and entered.

"Hola," a young woman said"How can I help you?"

"I represent a client who is interested in making a sizeable investment in some property," Harris answered, "What do you have that's available?"

"Any particular location?" "On the beach, definitely." "What's your client's price range?"

"Price is not an issue, I'm looking for something big."

"I have some listings for properties between 2200 and 2700 square feet."

"No, no, no I'm looking for something much bigger."

"I don't have any current listings for anything-larger than 2700. There are some new homes that were built recently in the 3200 to 4000 square foot range, but none of them are currently on the market"
"No I'm looking for something much larger. My client has money to spend and he wants a resort."

"There is vacant land available on the North end of the island. He could build something in the 5000-10,000 square foot range with deep water access and a swimming pool. I'm afraid that's the only way he'll get what he's looking for."

"You're still not understanding me. We're looking for something huge--something palatial-I'm talking in the 20,000 to 25,000 square foot range."

"Sir, there's only one house of that size on this island, and it is definitely not for sale."

"Can you get me in touch with the owner? Perhaps if I make him an offer, we could come to some sort of an agreement. Of course, you would still be entitled to your commission as the procuring cause of the transaction. We won't cut you out."

"That property is not for sale I'm sorry, but we are closing now. You'll have to come back tomorrow"
"Of course where did you say that property is located?"

"On the north end, but I'm warning you, do not try to contact the owner. He does not like to be disturbed. He has the means to make your life difficult if you intrude upon his privacy."

"Oh, I'm sure I've heard about the idiosyncracies of these reclusive billionaires. My client is like that, too no problem. I have some properties in Costa Rica and Jamaica to look at, so I'll be on my way- Thank you for your time."

The staircase leading to the cellar was located just off the main kitchen. Dana and Na exited the armory and headed in that direction each had an K-47 slung over her shoulder and was carrying a 9mm handgun with silencer. Na selected those weapons because she and Micaela had trained. Dana in their use over the last ten days.

Two guards were stationed outside the doorway leading to the stairs Na and Dana hid around a corner, less than forty feet away Na motioned to Dana, indicating that she would take out the guard on the left and Dana was to take out the guard on the right. Na signaled a silent count, and on three, the women stepped into the hallway. Each fired a single round, dropping the two guards in their places.

Alexander had little trouble locating the compound. The information from the realtor pointed him in the general vicinity, and once he was in the area he found the only one road leading in that direction. When he reached the end of the mile-long cul-de-sac, he discovered that the property was surrounded by a fifteen foot wall with surveillance cameras mounted at regular intervals. He drove past the gate without slowing. Half-mile down the road, Harris found a gap in the brush, he turned his car into the shaded area and parked. The dense foliage overhead and on three sides hid him from all but the most observant eyes. Alexander pulled out a map and studied the area, his reconnaissance informed him that the security wall shielded the property on three sides. The ocean protected the fourth side. The only way to breach the perimeter would be through an amphibious assault. Even with proper equipment, that would be a near impossibility in the daytime. In any event, that was a moot point. He didn't have the proper equipment.

Harris took out his binoculars and stepped into the road. Looking to the east and south, he saw dense foliage that provided great cover, but no means of getting past the security cameras mounted on the compound walls. To the north was all sea and beach. The sun headed toward the mountains in the west, which were dotted with large homes along the winding road leading to the peak set, those homes would be swallowed up by the shadows of the mountain peak what he had to do.

By the time, the sun suddenly, Harris knew Dana opened the door leading to the cellar stair-Wayna stepped into the breach, spotted the guard, and fired.

The man at the bottom of the stairs fell to the floor as blood spurted from the hole in his forehead.

The two women hurried down the stairs. Na searched the guard's body. She removed a hand gun, which she handed to Dana. Dana reached over her shoulder and tucked the gun between her bra strap and her spine. Na pulled a key ring from the guard's pants pocket and examined it. When she found the proper key, she handed it to Dana.

Dana took her position in front of the door, while Na crouched next to the door jamb. Dana turned the key and pulled the door open. Na jumped into the opening, acquired her target, and froze Harris made two phone calls, and then drove to a dive shop in the business district. There weren't many places to purchase what he needed on the island, and he was surprised to find the closest vendor was better known for selling scuba gear. Two one hundred dollar bills convinced the clerk that Harris was certified in the use of the equipment he wanted to purchase. The man didn't ring up the sale on his cash register, and he insisted that the transaction be completed in cash.

Thirty minutes later, Harris loaded everything into the back seat, trunk, and roof of his rental car, and drove to the top of the mountain. "Come in," Hernandez said" I wasn't expecting both of you. But seeing the two of you, two tells me everything I need to know."

Na and Dana stepped inside the doorway. Both women aimed their K-47s at Hernandez, who was standing in the far corner of the room. His pants were bunched around his knees, and his erect cock jutted from his groin. Micaela was beneath him, kneeling on the floor with her arms chained around a toilet. Her head was in the bowl and the seat was resting on her shoulders.

Hernandez held a taser in his left hand. Two darts were stuck in Micaela's back. He was also holding a 9mm hand gun against Micaela's head. His semen was leaking out of her ass and dripping onto the floor.

"So, the traitor finally reveals herself" The smug tone of his voice infuriated Dana "I knew if I put the two of you together in the same room the truth would emerge."

"What are you talking about?" Na demanded "We're not the traitors. Let my sister go, and I'll give you a quick death. If you hurt her, I promise you it will be slow and painful."

"You aren't the traitor I was referring to, Na's for your sister, well, she's alive but she'll require medical attention. I'm not familiar with the specifications of this particular taser, but if your sister lives, I'm sure she'll be able to tell you all about them."

"You fucking asshole," Na screamed" Let her go Now."

"Not until we have resolved the matter of the traitor in our midst."

"Why do you keep saying that?"

"Ask Lydia--she can tell you or should I say, ask Dana?"

Hernandez inched away from Micaela, he couldn't walk with his pants bunched around his knees, but he had a weapon in each hand and refused to relinquish his hold on either.

"What's he talking about, Lydia?" Na asked.

"This morning we were all meeting on the yacht- Jorge, Mateo, Franklin, and myself Franklin found a bug. I planted it."

"You?" turned her weapon toward Dana

"Why?"

"I was working undercover for the Miami Police Department."

"You're a cop?" Na's voice reverberated throughout the room. "I was," Dana answered "But I'm not anymore."

"You've been lying this entire time. You caused all of this! I should kill you."

"Take her gun," Hernandez said.

"Drop your weapon!" Na ordered "Do what he says."

"Na, listen to me, he's going to kill all three of us.

It's the only way he can justify all the dead bodies" "Shut your mouth, traitor! On the ground!" Dana set the AK-47 on the floor reach.

"On your knees!" Na commanded.

Na took a step toward her and then kicked the weapon out of Dana's

"Now!"

Dana slowly dropped to her knees. She put her hands behind her head and looked up at Na. "Na,"

Dana pleaded "I can explain."

"Shut your fucking mouth, whore, Na said." My sister and I had a good thing here. This organization was going to be our future. Our lives had a purpose. You destroyed it. You destroyed everything. I should blow your fucking head off."

Na pressed the barrel of her gun against Dana's temple.

"Tell me why I don't kill you now. Or would you prefer that I let Hernandez finish you off his way?" "I saved your life, Na."

Na hit Dana in the head with the butt of her rifle, opening a cut on her forehead purple lump formed and blood trickled down her face.

"Fuck you! You were saving your own life at least, that's what you thought. Well, whore, your life expectancy can now be measured in hours. Maybe I'll just wait a little while longer and let Las Casas decide how he wants to handle you."

From an elevation of 500 feet, Harris spotted the compound a half mile in the distance. Soaring in from the west, he did his best to remain on a direct line with the compound and the setting sun. If everything went according to plan, no one would see his approach or his attempt to land the hang glider on the roof of the house.

He should have known that successfully executing his plan would require more than mere luck. The instructional videos he pulled up on Youtube were informative, but it still took seven attempts at jumping off the mountain before he was able to get into the air. His crashes on attempts two and four were especially painful, but his equipment was undamaged and Dana was still in danger, so he continued trying as he approached the compound. Harris attempted to maneuver himself into position for a landing on the center of the roof the last second he realized he still had too much velocity, so he pulled up to avoid crashing into the steeply sloped tile. He cleared the apex, but when he tried to bank around and come back for a second pass, he no longer had sufficient altitude to land on top of the house. Instead, he found himself gliding to the ground near the dock.

Alexander crumpled to the grass just as gunshots whizzed over his head. He disengaged himself from the glider and rolled to his left. He saw a man standing on the pier aiming his handgun. Alexander drew his weapon and shot. The man fell off the dock and splashed into the water. Harris took cover underneath the dock.

He heard voices overhead, followed by footsteps man with an automatic weapon jumped off the dock and ran toward the hang glider. He poked it with his foot and then turned toward the dock. Harris fired, and the man collapsed on the grass, another set of footsteps ran across the wooden deckman suddenly appeared in the sand next to the supports. Harris kicked before the man could fire a shot. His foot struck the man's groin, crushing his balls. The man doubled over in pain. Harris fired, hitting the man in the back of his head.

Harris waited several seconds. He didn't hear any more voices or footsteps. He took a quick look around, and then made his way to back entrance of the house.

Stepping inside, Harris heard only silence cautiously making his way through the house. Harris took note of the dead bodies littering the hallways.

The first ones he encountered had their throats slit, but the corpses he found on the second floor had their skulls bashed. Whoever was responsible for the carnage was adept with a variety of weapons.

After finishing his tour of the second floor and finding no sign of Dana, Harris resumed his search of the first floor. He spotted two dead bodies at the end of a long hallway--both with bullet holes in their foreheads--and was heading in that direction when he heard a gunshot. Alexander threw caution to the wind and sprinted for the door flanked by the two corpses.

"Do you have anything I can use to blind this whore?" Na asked.

"There's a coil of rope in that cabinet" Hernandez pointed toward some wooden built-ins on the opposite wall. "There's also some razor wire over there if you look around, you should be able to find some leather gloves, and a pair of wire cutters."

"If I use the razor wire she'll probably bleed out before Las Casas gets here."

"That's her problem, not yours."

"It's our problem, Mateo I'm sure that Las Casas will want to decide for himself the fate of his favorite whore--after he questions her. She needs to be breathing when he gets here."

"I wouldn't worry so much about Las Casas if I were you. Thanks to that fucking whore, I'm afraid his days are numbered."

"And then who's taking over? You?"

"Who else? Franklin? Give me a break, I don't even think I could realistically promote him to my number two. Who does that leave? The two of you?" "You won't have to worry about us soon as this whore is secure, I'm getting my sister and we're getting the fuck out of here. Do you have a problem with that?"

"No." "Good."

Na stood up and took two steps to her right.

"Mateo!" she called.

Hernandez' eyes darted from Micaela to Na in that instant, Dana slid her hand down the back of her shirt, grabbed the pistol tucked into her bra strap, and drew it, she fired one shot.

Hernandez dropped his gun red spot spread across the front of his shirt. He coughed up blood, and then fell forward. His head hit the ground with a sickening thud.

"Get your sister and get out of here," Dana said, Na hurried over to Micaela, she lifted the toilet seat off her head, pulled the taser darts out of her back, and started cutting away her ropes.

"How is she?" Dana asked.

"She's breathing, but she's unconscious I think she has internal injuries. She's beaten pretty bad."

"Finish getting those ropes off her while I go find her some clothes I'll be right--"

The door burst open.

"Freeze!"

Dana turned and saw Alexander standing inside the door, pointing two K-47s.

"Stand down, Levan they're with me." "Dana! You're alive!"

"You know him?" Na asked.

"He's the person who got me into all this." "I'm Detective Harris."

"How did you find me? Are you alone? Where's your back up?"

"I'm a detective, remember? And I don't have any back up. This mission is solo."

"And unapproved, right? No matter, I'm glad you're here, Harris I'm going to get some clothes for Micaela, and then I need for you to take the twins and get them to a hospital. Micaela needs to be checked out."

"We can't go to a hospital on the island," Na said." Las Casas will find us."

"How did you get here, Levan?" Dana asked.

"We're not getting out the way I came in."

"Then we only have one option Levan, do you think you can pilot a yacht?" "I supposes oh Why?" "You're taking Crespo's yacht. It's slightly less conspicuous than Las Casas' ocean liner. You can be in Cozumel before dawn." "What about you?"

"I'll meet you there tomorrow, but first, I have some unfinished business" "I'm not leaving you here, Dana."

"Yes, you now start preparing for departure, you need to be as far from here as possible when Las Casas arrives."

"Dana, I didn't come all the way out here just to leave without you."

"I appreciate that Levan, but I can take care of myself marina over three weeks ago I don't need to be rescued.

I'm not the same person you dropped off at the- What I do need is for you to take my friends and get them out of here. I'll meet up with you tomorrow. I promise, now go."

Dana was seated at the conference table when Las Casas entered the house. She had opened a bottle of his best wine, which was sitting on the table with two Bordeaux glasses.

"What happened here?" Las Casas spoke in a crisp staccato rhythm, emphasizing every syllable "There are bodies everywhere."

"Sit down, Jorge let me pour you a drink."

Las Casas took a seat Dana poured two glasses of wine "Where's Mateo?"

"He's in the cellar, he's dead." "And the twins?"

"They're gone."

"They killed Hernandez and escaped?"

"No, I killed Hernandez and I let them go."

"You what?" Las Casas' eyes bulged. He pulled a gun from his waist and pointed it at Dana's forehead "I killed him," Dana said, "to save your life."

"My life? How?"

"Hernandez was plotting to kill you and take over your business. His hand has been behind everything that happened here in the past 24 months."

Dana paused to take a sip of her wine.

"Crespo never stole from you," she continued "Hernandez set him up once Crespo was out of the way, you were the next target. He was going to take you out as soon as you stepped off the helicopter."

"Then what about the bug? Why did he place it on my boat? Was he working with Torres?"

"I planted the bug, the twins and Torres had nothing to do with any of this."

"You? Why?"

"I was working with the police, they put me on the boat for the purpose of planting the bug."

"What information have you provided them?" "Nothing, I didn't place it until the day after the party. The battery died before you were ever in that room again. They got nothing from it."

"If everything you are telling me is true, then I have no choice but to kill you."

"I expected you to say that, I had hoped that you wouldn't, but I knew you would. It's your nature" "I'm a businessman, your actions have compromised my entire enterprise."

Dana turned her face as a tear rolled down her cheek. She took a long sip of wine and then continued.

"I have an offer for you."

"I'm listening."

"I'll give you everything the Miami-Dade Police

Department has on you if you'll let me leave. Their complete files are yours if you just agree to let me go and promise to never contact me again."

"You could have been my wife, Lydia I would have married you."

"It's Dana my Name is Dana and no, I couldn't. This life isn't for me. I was scared and I was desperate, and tried to convince myself that somehow, someway,

I could become what you wanted me to be. But becoming that person would have meant no longer being myself, I can't do it."

"Dana Dana Dana, you place me in a difficult position more than anything else, I just want to turn back the clock and start this day all over again. I want you at my side and in my bed forever. I want to show you the world. I want to give you the world. You are the first woman for whom I have ever cared enough to envision a future together. But now? The safest option for me is to kill you."

"Listen to yourself, Jorge one second you're saying you care for me, that you want me to be your wife, and then the next that you have to kill me because it's what's best for you. Damn it, Jorge, do you care for me or not?"

"Of course, I care for you. I just don't know how I can trust you."

"If you ever loved me, you'll let me go" Dana reached for Las Casas' hand and pressed the barrel of the gun against her forehead" If not, then shoot me."

Dana closed her eyes and sobbed. Tears rolled down her cheeks, but she held her head steady against the gun barrel.

"Make a choice, Jorge either shoot me, or let me go."

Las Casas stared at Dana for several seconds. He ground his teeth together and beads of sweat formed on his temple. He pulled the gun away and set it on the table tear ran down his cheek.

"Go," he said "Get out." "Thank you, Jorge, thank you."

Dana jumped up and wrapped her arms around Las Casas, she kissed him on the forehead, but when he tilted his face and looked up at her, she pressed her lips against his. Dana reached into her pocket and pulled out a scrap of paper.

"The twins left on Crespo's yacht. In seven days, the boat will be at these coordinates in the Dry Tortugas, approximately twelve miles north of Fort Jefferson. Be there at noon. The files will be on the boat. Everything will be there I promise. You'll have to rebuild your organization, but with this information, you can do it smarter and faster. If you make it leaner, you can surpass where you were in a matter of months."

"Goodbye, Dana."

"Goodbye, Jorge."

Dana hurried out of the house. She jumped into a car and drove to the airport, where she contacted a US Consulate and spent the rest of the night arranging for travel documents and an airline ticket. The next morning she took the first flight to Cozumel, where she met up with Harris and the twins.

"Detectives," Captain Hendricks said to the two men standing in his office "Have a seat."

Alexander and Espinoza sat in the two chairs placed in front of the Captain's desk. Both men fidgeted as they waited for the Captain to speak.

"I just got off the phone with my contact at the DE," Hendricks announced, "He shared some remarkable news with me. Can either of you guess what that might be?"

"No, Sir," both men answered.

"Prepare yourselves to be shocked. We finally got some justice Crespo is dead."

"Are you sure?" Alexander asked, "How?" Zac added.

"According to sources, Las Casas executed him. It appears that Crespo was preparing to make a move on Las Casas, but the bastard found out first and took out Crespo before he could implement his plan. The son of a bitch shot him in cold blood in front of his wife, mother and sister. Then he turned the gun on them and wiped out the whole fucking family."

"That's great news," Espinoza said "Have you passed this on to Yolanda?" "I haven't had the chance. The call just came in five minutes ago."

"Do you mind if I'm the one to tell her?" Zac asked" I think she should hear it in person" "By all means."

"I'll head over to her house right now" Espinoza stood up and left the room. Alexander got out of his seat and was following Zac to the door when the Captain stopped him. "Sit down, Alexander."

"Sir?"

"Internal affairs is dropping its investigation into that surveillance video of you beating some man behind that warehouse. They couldn't identify the victim because the resolution was too low. Since no one came in and filed a complaint against you, they couldn't build much of a case."

"That's great, am I off desk duty now?" "No."

"No?"

"That's right I can't make a case against you, but I can't unsee what I saw. I watched one of my best detectives lose his head and pistol whip an unarmed man. Your pathetic explanations of 'gambling debts' and 'teaching a punk a lesson' don't wash with me, so I'm suspending you for two weeks without pay.

When you come back, you're on desk duty for two more weeks to that point, I'll consider reinstating your privileges."

"Understood, Is that all, Sir?"

"Just one more thing, that missing Cadet, Mslvarado, finally turned up. It seems that she was out of the country on some family business--in Cuba, I think, is what she told her instructors anyway, she's been asked to re-enter the cade by next year, but she says she's no longer interested. Have either you or Espinoza spoken to her?"

"No, Sir."

"That behaviour is kind of strange, don't you think? She was at the top of her class."

"People change, Sir."

"I'd sure like to know what caused that kind of change. Six weeks ago, I met someone who I was certain would eventually be one of the best cops in this department. Now, no interest at all… Go figure."

"Sometimes we experience things or lose things that change who we are. Sometimes those losses create wounds that never heal, or scars that never fade. If we could go back and undo what we did, we would--in a heartbeat."

"That's rather deep, Detective."

"Just thinking about some of my decisions and what I've lost, Sir."

"Go home, Harris I'll see you in two weeks."

"Goodbye, Captain."

After quitting her chance of getting back to the academy as a cadet, Yuonna started her small restaurant business.

Rebuilding his empire was the easiest thing for Jorge but he could not forget the woman who broke him.

His undercover love YUONNA!

THE

END